Adrift in the Sea
Of Souls

by

David Gerrold

D1737175

Trade paperback ISBN: 9798672410395

Creative Director: Kermit Woodall.

Editor in Chief: Ira Nayman

Associate Editors: Judith K. Dial, Lloyd Penney.

Amazing Stories, *Amazing Selects* and their logos are wholly owned trademarks of Experimenter Publishing Company, LLC. Visit us online at **amazingstories.com**.

Second edition.

Table of Contents

For Kent Youngblood, with love

Introduction: The Sprung Chicken

by
Adam-Troy Castro

David Gerrold is an old man.

Now, I happen to have written other introductions to short story collections in my life, including at least one prior volume of his, and I am very much aware that this a rude way to talk about somebody.

When you write an intro to an author's book, you are supposed to say things about their towering genius and sterling character, and how they are the most memorable person you have ever met, and that one time in the resistance when the two of you were fleeing the Nazis and he supported your wounded ass all the way past the razor wire and into Switzerland, and never even begrudged you that extra schnitzel, plus swept up afterward, and he plays a mean violin too.

You are not supposed to begin your testimonial with the observation that so-and-so is an old man, because that's rude, or perceived as rude, which is, in many contexts, the same thing.

(To that point: an author I admired quite a bit, meaning well, once submitted an introduction for an early collection of mine saying that I was odd, that I was socially inept, that I was unwashed, that I creeped people the fuck out, and that I sure could write; that was thirty years ago, and it was not incredibly delusional about the version of me that existed at the time, except possibly the "sure could write" part, not yet... It was not a tribute any writer would have wanted to appear as the intro to his showcase, so I refused to use it. What a memory. I am hoping that David and company read enough of this one to put the "He's old" opener in proper context.)

By the calendar alone, the statement happens to be true.

This is just the way time works.

He made his first big splash over fifty years ago, via a cultural touchstone that I am going to break the usual pattern of David Gerrold introductions by not specifically mentioning. He has gray hair. He grumps about telling the kids to stay off his lawn. He is, at this writing, eagerly awaiting the arrival of his first grandchild. And he is no longer that "skinny kid" you see in some contemporary references: not, you know, as rounded as the egg-shaped yours truly, but certainly not fodder for the memorable description of him I once read by somebody from way back when as a guy whose body type and nose made him resemble a crowbar. (I am nagged by the suspicion that David wrote it of himself.) He is, and frequently describes himself as, an old man, a curmudgeon who tells the kids to stay off his lawn. He may be taken aback that I begin this introduction with that statement of fact, but he will not deny it.

And now let me tell you about the other attributes that are frequently attributed to old men.

They are alleged to be cranky.

They are alleged to be hidebound.

They are alleged to be set in their ways.

They are alleged to have their greatest achievements behind them.

They are alleged to be tired, strangers to the children they once were.

In David's case, I will cop to the "cranky." So will he. Frequently. I sometimes think he uses it pre-emptively, to make sure nobody else says it before he can. Many, many of his social media pronouncements end with him conceding that yes, "cranky" fits, and again, reminding you damn kids to get off his lawn. He does keep saying that.

But everything else –

Holy Jumping Moons of Saturn, that is so **not** him.

Let us talk first about "hidebound, out of touch, set in their ways." After that prominent debut in a venue that has since become claimed by the most hidebound minds as the model for the one true pew-pew-pew model of science fiction, he demonstrated that he was not only interested in writing fiction set in places which have control panels that light up. Sure, he had one foot in the land that Campbell and Asimov and especially Heinlein colonized, and when he wanted to, he could step back in and inhabit that landscape as well as any other talent you could name, as in, among other places, his Chtorr novels, but when he wanted to he also visited the lands of literary experimentation and wrote stories like "In the Deadlands," "With A Finger In My I," and that early, splendid, trail-blazing time travel novel, *The Man Who Folded Himself.* Then, after he wrote them, he could return, via collaboration with Larry Niven, to work that was so Asimovian that it had a version of Asimov as a character, *The Flying Sorcerers.*

"Hidebound?" Hardly. He never, ever became that one. Nor "set in (his) ways." No one in the field has written a novel more stylistically audacious, as jaw-dropping, as his *Thirteen Fourteen Fifteen O'Clock*, published a mere five years ago and very, very bloody different from his most recent, *Hella*, a strong planetary-colonization novel of which it could be said that even if it took David to write it, Heinlein himself would certainly recognize his own DNA.

An attribute of many writers I love, of Harlan, of Sheckley, of Twain in fact, of Dan Simmons and of newer talents like Charlie Jane Anders and Nora Jemisin and Sarah Pinsker, is that when you see their bylines, you may be able to mine your memories of past work to guess what the newest story will be like, but you will never be able to tell for **sure** until you break the seal and start reading. David has always been like that. Who the hell expected a piece like "The White Piano" from him at this late date? That's not the kind of story you expect from **David Gerrold**. It's not that mythical beast, **A David Gerrold Story**. And yet there it is, and when he writes another it is equally likely that it will be that creature known as "A David Gerrold Story" and "A Story that You Never Expected from David Gerrold," the secret being that the only difference between one category and the other is the reader's preset expectation.

It's one chief reason why "their greatest achievements behind them" is another old-man signifier that doesn't apply in David Gerrold's case. Honestly, if there's one thing I'm not gonna say about Aged Artist X – I can think of several possible people in this category – is that I expect their next work to blow everything done before out of the water. Many operate at the level described by Randy Newman in the song, "I'm Dead (But I Don't Know It)," when his aged pop-star character sings, "Every record that I make / sounds like a record that I made / just not as good." If Mick Jagger, one possible model for that character, announces the release of a new song tomorrow, you somehow don't expect it to be the best thing he's done in the past fifty years. You don't. It might be good, but it won't be **surprising**. You don't expect that.

And yet David has surprised me **recently**, with "Bubble and Squeak," a *tour de force* novella written with Ctein.

It's not only possible but **likely**, nay, **probable**, that he will again.

If somebody in the know says to me of a David Gerrold story coming out next month that it's one of the best things he's ever done, I will be excited, but I will not be astonished; I will say, based on recent and current evidence, that it always was a possibility. Okay? Witness the stories here as exhibit one.

And then we come to the last signifier of old men, that they are supposed to be strangers to the children they once were.

Have you even **met** David?

I mentioned earlier that he is expecting a grandchild, and what I promise you is that the kid will not come to think of Gramps as the basically immobile old fart who must be acknowledged, resentfully kissed on the cheek and then not bothered for the rest of the day. David is an adult who has known tragedy, adulation, responsibility, personal dedication to family, and the ten million forms of radioactive *tsuris* that afflict the adult animal, but "jaded" he is not. Spend any time with him and you will know his primal nature: that in his heart he's about twelve. His new descendant will think of him accordingly.

In short, anybody who really knows him understands that he's **still** one of the kids who won't stay off the lawn.

This is why his work remains vital and important and why he remains a source of light.

Enjoy.

Adam-Troy Castro
July, 2020

Publisher's Note: David Gerrold

by
Steve Davidson

For the next few moments, I want you to cast your mind back to the time of your own personal Golden Age of Science Fiction. Maybe you were 10, or 12, or 16. Maybe, comparatively speaking, that was yesterday, or maybe, like it is for me, it was decades ago.

Do you remember how you felt? Oh, probably not in crystal clear detail, but I am sure you remember the feelings. Awe. Excitement. Wonder. Anticipation. A dash of annoyance that it took so long to discover these treasures. A hint of jealous protectiveness. A near uncontrollable desire to scream and shout its existence at the heart of the world. The near-certain knowledge that you possessed the keys that would unlock your future.

Now, I want you to imagine that you are attending a convention. You're standing at a bank of elevators in the lobby of a hotel, far from home, surrounded by friendly strangers (all of whom seem a bit odd – but no odder than yourself) when the door of one of the elevators opens and there stands David Gerrold. Not David Gerrold as you know him now. David Gerrold as you **didn't** know him back then.

A youngish looking man with an infectious grin. An approaching middle-aged man wearing badge ribbons that clearly identify him as a guest of the convention. An (hushed, with reverence) *AUTHOR*.

And in this case, not just *an* author. A legendary one. One responsible not only for words in books, but also for images and dialogue on television and the big screen.

OMG! (this is an anachronism: OMG was not an expression all of those decades ago), it's **that** guy who wrote one of your favorite episodes of **that** TV show!

No one moved to get off that elevator. David held the door and invited me in, (invited me IN!) apparently aware that I had been shocked into immobility by his very presence.

I cautiously entered, carefully avoiding physical contact with The Presence. One does not casually brush shoulders with the Great Ones. True, we'd made eye contact and I was still alive to tell the tale, but fate should not be tempted.

David pressed the button for the top floor. The doors hushed closed. As the numbers on the display ticked towards the last stop, everyone in the elevator crouched. As the car began to slow, they gathered themselves and hopped, floating for a brief moment of earthbound weightlessness, smiles, cheers and claps all around.

I had just been introduced to Elevator Racing as well as, incidentally, David Gerrold.

It seems that these were express elevators and, if you got a clear run from the lobby to the penthouse suites, they built up enough momentum so that a good hop would buy you some noticeable float, like the rise you get at the top of a rollercoaster.

David's fiction has been giving me that rise ever since. From *The Flying Sorcerers* (with Larry Niven) to *The Martian Child*, from Tribbles to Sleestaks,

David Gerrold has been part of my science fiction landscape since my own Golden Age. Preceded only by *Fireball XL-5*, *Jonny Quest* and *Voyage to the Bottom of the Sea*, contemporary with *Lost in Space* and Heinlein. And whether you know it or not, David has been a part of your science fiction landscape for just as long, if not longer.

That's how long he's been at this. Television shows, films, articles, stories, novels, series. And a lot of talking to and with audiences, advocating, encouraging, understanding, instructing *and* correcting.

Always with love and compassion.

It gives me great pleasure as not only a publisher, but as a Fan, to be able to bring this collection of David Gerrold stories to you.

Now stop gawking and push that button for the top floor – we're going UP!

Steve Davidson
Hillsboro NH
July, 2020

Adrift in the Sea of Souls

I woke up hurting and crying. I was small and dirty, all curled into a ball. Everything smelled bad. I smelled bad. Everything was dark. I couldn't even see myself. I felt around and found my blankie. It was stiff and crusty and stinky. I wrapped myself up in it anyway. But I was still cold. I shivered a lot.

And my head hurt, too. Not like somebody hitting me from the outside. I knew that a lot. This was like somebody hitting me from the inside. It hurt in a different way.

I remembered hate. A big hot hate, so big it burned all bright like the hurt at the center of the sky. I was screaming and screaming so hard, I was on fire. "I don't want to be me anymore –"

And then, I wasn't.

I was here. In the smelly dark.

And cold. I was cold. A long time cold. My feet were so cold, they hurt. My fingers were stiff and clumsy. I didn't want to move because when I did, the cold got under my blanket and that hurt even more. I shivered a lot. But I had to get up and move because it hurt too much to stay where I was. The floor was hard and cold. But I pushed myself over anyway. My stomach hurt. My arms hurt. My fingers were hard to move. My legs hurt, too. I couldn't see anything, my eyes felt gritty, it hurt to rub them, I squinched them tight.

I rolled over. I bumped into a wall. I was so shaky. I leaned against the wall and pulled myself up. I almost fell, but I leaned against the wall with both hands. I pushed my feet under me and stood. The wall was old paint, it was chipped and peeling. I worked my way sideways, feeling carefully until I bumped into a corner. I bumped into a stinky bucket too. It was a bad smell. But I had to pee.

I wasn't naked. I had a big shirt on. It smelled, too. It hung down below my knees. I had to pull it up so I could squat over the bucket. The body knew what to do. This wasn't the first time. Eventually, I realized I was through. I straightened. Not easily. Still holding the front of my shirt up to my neck, I looked down at myself –

Oh.

I am a child. A small, brown child. A small, brown, female child.

Part of me was almost able to understand. But I was drowning in pain. It pulled me down into it. Swallowing me. The hurt so great, I fell down crying. I stumbled against the wall. I just wanted to go back to my corner.

This wasn't me. Not the self that had been screaming.

I was in a tiny room. Not much bigger than a closet. Some kind of storeroom. There was a small window at the very top of one wall. Only a little light. One corner had a pile of rags – my bed. Another corner had a bucket of stinky filth – my toilet. There was a door. The doorknob was level with my eyes. I tried it anyway. It was locked.

This much. I knew this much. Whoever was on the other side of that door, they were horrible.

I collapsed to the floor, crying. Part of it was the pain of the body. All the hurt. It just wouldn't stop. Part of it was me. Frail and helpless and trapped.

This four-year-old brain didn't have the words. The body was fighting me, too. It didn't like me –

Fair enough. I didn't like me either.

But here we were.

Both of us.

Curled up inside a ball of pain. Me and the other me. The hurting little me.

That little me was a small dark thing, given up, resigned, a silent presence shrunk inside itself, a shriveled kernel of the soul born here.

I am only borne here. An intruder. An invader.

Souls need nourishment to grow. This little one hadn't.

Deprive a soul of light, it doesn't die, but it doesn't grow either. It shrivels, it shrinks, it withdraws into a tiny cold nugget of existence that endures until the body finally dies and there is nothing more to endure.

"Hello –?"

It didn't answer. Maybe it blinked. Maybe it looked up for the briefest instant. I couldn't tell.

"How long have you been locked up in here?"

It doesn't answer. The answer is forever.

"I know it hurts. I've been hurt, too. Maybe I can help –?"

Still nothing. It doesn't care. It gave up caring a long time ago.

"Hello? Please. Let's get out, okay?"

It doesn't believe in out. There is no out.

"Please talk to me. I won't hurt you. I'm – I'm a friend."

No. Nothing.

It isn't going to trust me. Why should it? It's never known anything but pain and fear.

"Please talk to me. I'm scared, too. Please?"

No response.

It's a trap. The more I try to get inside it, the more it owns me.

This thing here, this small curdle of existence, I mustn't get sucked into it.

I can't do anything here. I have to get out.

Pound on the door. A long time.

Nothing happened.

Pound and pound and pound and finally collapse against the hard cold wood, my fingers scrabbling helplessly through the trash scattered across the floor.

I cry. Not the body, no. Not the tiniest piece of soul that was festering down at the bottom of the dark. That part had given up crying a long time ago. No, this was me crying. The part that shouldn't be here.

I want to crawl inside the little me and hide there too.

No. Don't go there.

Endure.

After forever, a noise.

The door opened. The light on the other side was too bright, but something huge blocked the way. I'd never seen a giant before, a giant woman-thing, she kicked me hard out of the way – "What did I say about not making any more noise!" I scrambled back away from her. Not fast enough. She kicked me back into the corner, pushing me through all the dirt and filth on the floor. She slapped a metal bowl of something down. Dog food. Barely a scoop. "Lucky to get this, you are. You'll never be worth anything, I don't know why we do this –"

And then she was gone, slamming the door shut behind her. The locks clicked into place.

Now I knew where all the physical pain had come from – it was all the sideways shoves and slaps, all the deliberate kicks and blows and beatings, all of it was burned into this body like a smoldering brand. I curled up into a ball of hurt, until it hurt so much I had to uncurl.

I wanted away from here, away from me –

There was something in my hand. Something from the floor. Crumpled paper.

Paper was important. Even little me knew that.

I don't know why I unfolded it. Big me wanted to know.

There was no picture here, just crawly little insect marks. I could barely make them out in the gloom.

Wait.

Letters. Words.

Little me can't read. The paper makes no sense. But the other part, the part that didn't belong here, that part remembered an earlier time, a time when it could read.

Letters and words. It was an old bill for something. An address. I was in the dark at Courtney Pl – the rest was ripped.

Despair is a heavy weight. It pulls me down into the cold dark sea. All the way down to where the light no longer reaches and I will be crushed into nothing by the pressure.

I had to get angry instead.

Screaming angry.

A rage as big as the sky –

Bigger –

A big hot hate, so big it burned all dazzle-bright, bigger than the world, bigger than me. Scream and scream so hard, I'm on fire. I felt guilty leaving little me behind, but, "I don't want to be here any more –"

And then the scream exploded and I wasn't.

I popped.

I woke up, exhausted. Hurting from the glare.

Light everywhere.

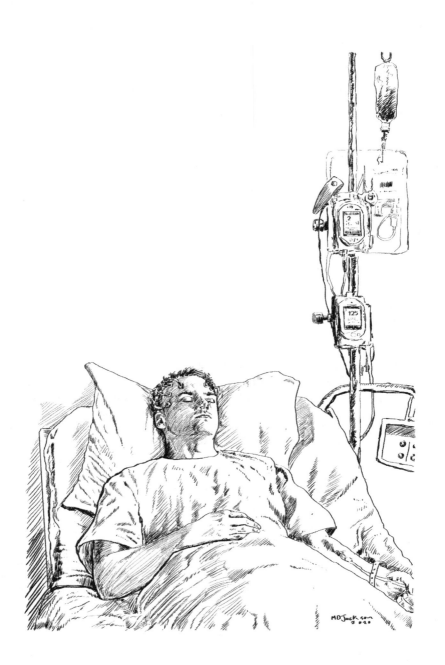

A blurry figure hovers over me. Another blurry figure behind.

I manage to croak some words. "Who am I –?"

"That's interesting. Most people ask, 'Where am I?'"

"I'm in a hospital. Right?" My voice is raspy. Male? Female? I can't tell. I'm still sorting myself out.

"You were in a coma."

"Unh. How long?"

"Ten days. Almost eleven. You surprised us. You were almost brain dead. Almost, not quite."

"I was –"

– not going to explain.

The doctor studied me. "How do you feel?"

"Um." I tried to swallow. I couldn't. "Thirsty."

"Understandable." She gestured to the nurse. He was a big black man. He handed me a plastic cup with ice in it. "Can you manage that?" she asked. "Or do you need help?"

"I think I can –" No, I couldn't. It felt hard to move my arm. My hand trembled. The nurse helped me sit up, guided the cup to my mouth.

The ice was a shock – but a delicious one. Three lifetimes of relief.

I closed my eyes, remembering. I almost dropped the cup, but the nurse caught it, handed it back to me. "Take it easy," he said.

The doctor waited patiently while I chewed a piece of ice. "What do you remember?" she asked. She studied me through narrow eyes. I didn't want to answer her question. I looked at my feet. I looked at the walls. I looked at everything – all the machines around me, the tabs on my skinny chest, the wires and tubes, her blue shirt, and finally her nametag – Dr. Melanie Eberling. I looked at everything but her eyes. She was thin and leathery. She looked determined.

"What do you remember?" she repeated.

I cleared my throat. It still hurt. I sucked on another piece of ice. "Um..." I finally said, "Nothing. I don't remember anything." I shook my head. Someone's head. But there was no one else here. I looked. I was still looking. They weren't hiding. They were gone.

"Do you know your name?"

"I'm –" I stopped. Not that name, no. "Um, no." I looked at Dr. Eberling with honest confusion. "Who am I?"

"Let's wait on that one. Let's see what comes back." She gestured to the nurse. "I want you to try standing up. You're going to need some physical therapy. All that time in bed, your muscles have started to atrophy. Let's see how bad –"

The nurse helped me swing my legs to the floor, helped me stand. I wobbled unsteadily, then sank back down onto the bed.

"All right, that's a start. Can you sit up by yourself?"

"I think so."

When I moved, there were...not memories, but flashes of experience. The body had its own history. Muscle memories?

I had to figure this out. There were images here, recalls, but confused. I couldn't sort them.

"I was in an accident, wasn't I –?"

"No."

"What –?"

"What do you remember?"

"I don't remember anything –"

"You tried to kill yourself." She waited for my response.

I let her wait. I had to sit with this. Well, yes – I did try to kill myself. But that was two lives ago. This person, too? Was that why I was here?

Where was he?

Oh.

His name had been – ah. Shield. Shields. Richard. Richard Shields. But somebody called him Dick. No Dicky. He didn't like that. The more he insisted on Richard, the more they called him Dicky. Little Dicky. Icky Dicky. The quicker pricker licker. The whole spew came bubbling up. Ugly memories, all of them. His anguish still echoed inside this head –

"What are you feeling?"

"It hurts in here."

"Where?"

"In here." I touched my chest. "And here." My head.

"Mm-hm." She looked to the monitors. "I can give you something for that."

"No shots, please."

She shook her head. "No shots." Instead, she nodded to the nurse. He slapped a patch on my shoulder. "That should do it," she said.

I started to protest, tried to pick the patch off. "No. No sedatives. I think I need to think clearly –"

The nurse pushed my hand away. "It's not a sedative," the doctor said. "It's a calming agent. Are you hungry? We'll get you some food."

"Can I ask? How did I –?"

"You don't remember?"

"I don't –" I shook my head. It was my head now. Not his. He was gone.

Whatever it was, whatever he did, he must have left this body. Because whoever had lived here, he was gone. There was no one else.

Maybe that was why I fell into it so easily.

It almost felt…well, not comfortable, but I could wear it.

"Pills. An overdose. It would have been fatal. But your… boyfriend found you. I presume it was your boyfriend. Whoever called it in, he wasn't there when the paramedics arrived. Do you remember his name?"

"I don't remember anything." That was a lie. I was starting to get flickers of his past experiences. None of them pleasant. If this was his life, I could understand why he wanted to escape. And then, I remembered something else.

She peered at me. "What –?"

I didn't want to say it, but I had to. "There's a little girl. She's locked in a storeroom somewhere. Wait –" I closed my eyes to remember. "The address is 6027 Courtney Place. She's four years old. I don't know her name. She's wearing a T-shirt, nothing else. She's been locked up in that storeroom for as long as she can remember. Rescue her, and I'll tell you everything."

The doctor stared at me. "Don't go anywhere. I mean it. I'll be right back."

The nurse followed her out. I was glad they left. It gave me time to explore this body and its memories. The body might have been male, but the mind that had lived here, it hadn't known if it was male or female. There were troubled memories, way too many. I couldn't get more than flickers, but the emotions came flooding up easily.

The body was fatigued, a week and a half in bed, the muscles were weak from disuse, but there hadn't been much to start with. This body was frail.

Could I pop out? Would a firestorm of rage propel me from this body and into another one? Probably. But what body? Where? Another empty one? Or another where the owner had gone catatonic? At least, here, for the moment…I needed to wait.

When the doctor came back, she had a grim look on her face. She studied me for a long moment. "It's not possible to fake being brain-dead."

"Huh?"

"So how did you know about the little girl?"

"I just knew. Is someone going to get her –?"

"The police found her three days ago."

"Is she all right?"

Dr. Eberling hesitated. "I'm sorry –"

"Wait! What? Tell me."

"She was already dead when they found her."

"How?"

"Malnutrition. Abuse. Beatings. Take your pick. The people who did it – they're in jail."

I remembered the pain. I could still feel it. I had to catch my breath.

"Are you all right?"

I shook my head. "What was her name?"

"Tandy Jones."

Tandy Jones. I turned the words over in my head. Tandy Jones. She never had a chance. "It was the woman," I said. "She did it."

"How do you know that?"

"I just know it."

"Even though you were here?" She added, "Almost brain dead?"

"I was there."

Dr. Eberling's expression changed. Halfway between a frown and something else.

I swallowed hard. It hurt. "I was – inside. Inside her head."

"You're a body-traveler." It wasn't a question.

"May I have some more ice?"

She turned away for a moment, pouring more ice from a pitcher. I wondered if I could pop out before she turned back. Almost – I could almost feel the way, but not quite.

Dr. Melanie Eberling came back with a cup of ice. She waited while I sucked at it. When I finally handed it back, she said, "Listen to me. Listen carefully. Do not deny that you are a body-traveler. We expected you. This body was brain-dead. No one home. It was just waiting for you, or someone like you, to pop in."

I had to think about that.

Dr. Eberling put the cup of ice on a side tray. "Did you pick this body out? Or was it random?"

"Random," I admitted.

"So, you can't control it yet."

"I, um – no. I mean, maybe if I start screaming hard enough." I stopped before I said more.

"Don't do that." She put a hand on my shoulder. Her grip was firm – as if she could hold me in place by sheer will power. "That's why I gave you a calming agent. To keep you here. Don't try to pop out. Just don't."

I was still thinking about the word yet. That was interesting.

Dr. Eberling misinterpreted my silence. "You could hurt yourself. And you could hurt someone else."

I didn't want her to know what she had revealed. I rubbed my eyes so she wouldn't see what I was thinking.

"You're important," she said. "We want to know what you know."

"Um. We? Who's that? Who's we?"

"All of us here. The doctors. We know that body-travelers sometimes show up in cases like this – where a body is untenanted. Or where the tenant has gone into remission. You know that word? Good. Usually, the new tenants pretend amnesia. But you didn't. You were concerned about the little girl, Tandy Jones. So, that's a good thing. It shows you have compassion. And a conscience. We want to understand this phenomenon. You could answer a lot of questions. So please don't move on, promise me?"

"I don't think I have the strength to pop."

"Pop? Is that what you call it when you move from one body to another?"

"That's what it felt like, yes."

"Listen. If you'll help us, then we'll help you. First, we'll have to build up your strength. If you try to pop out, this body could die. And you might, too."

I didn't say anything. Silence was my only option. I really had to think about this. There was so much that I needed to know. I needed to know what they knew.

"How are you feeling right now?"

"I have to pee," I said.

"I'll call Kent. He's your nurse. If there's anything you need, press this button. I'll check on you first thing tomorrow."

And she did.

They started slow. Physical therapy, mostly. And a lot of protein. Then, more physical therapy. It was exhausting. This body was weak. But as soon as they could, they began the tests. A lot of tests. All kinds.

The cat scan wasn't so bad, but the MRI was painfully loud, even with the earplugs. They shaved the head of my new body and attached all kinds of EEG monitors. I didn't argue. I knew I was going to stay only as long as it was convenient. But this was interesting. I might learn something.

The physical therapy went from exhausting to painful. The muscles of this body were underdeveloped, weak even at the best of times, so that was another goal, get me healthy and fit –

– but Dr. Eberling also kept a careful watch on my moods. I wasn't allowed to get stressed or angry. The calming patch was replaced twice a day. I existed in a mellow haze of feel-good blurriness. There was no tuner for the TV in my room. It showed endless travelogues. I flew over forests, I swam through coral reefs, I drifted with clouds. All very peaceful.

It was a vacation from myself.

Except for the endless interviews. And tests. And all the questions I didn't want to answer.

"I wish you could trust us –"

"Why should I? I don't know what you're doing. I don't know what you want. And you won't let me leave; so really, if you think about it, I'm in prison here, aren't I? It's a very nice prison, but –"

"Yes, I can understand why you would feel that way. But we don't know who you really are, or where you came from, or how you got here. We do know that you're not Richard Shields –"

"You can't prove that I'm not Richard Shields. Maybe I am –"

"You've already admitted that you're not –"

"Maybe I was delusional –"

"Well, okay. If you want to go that way – we have two psychiatrists who are ready to certify that you're delusional. And that would be even more limiting for you."

"If you do that, I won't cooperate."

"You're not cooperating now."

"Why should I? I don't know what you're doing. Or why. You're not explaining anything –"

"Richard – I'll call you Richard, all right? Isn't it obvious what we're trying to do here? It's the mind-body problem with all of the existential questions that come with it. How much of you is your body? How much is mind? What is the mind? Oh hell, what is consciousness? And ultimately – is the soul immortal? Is it possible to leave our bodies and live as pure spirit? All we have are guesses – and a few urban legends. You represent a unique opportunity. You can answer a lot of questions for us. For all humanity. But let's start with the obvious one. How does body-traveling work? Is it controllable?"

"This is all for science? Really?"

"Yes," she said. "For science."

I didn't believe her.

She wasn't locking me in a closet and feeding me bowls of sour dog food – but it was a difference of degree, not of kind. I was still a captive. I had to endure. I had to wait it out. The more I built my strength up – the more I built up the strength of Richard Shields' frail body – the sooner I could get out.

But at the same time, the stronger I got, the more rigorous were the tests.

The physical tests weren't painful. They were just annoying. They took blood samples, urine and feces too. They took cheek swabs. They peered up my nostrils and into my ears. They flashed pictures of my retinas. They looked at hair and skin samples under electron microscopes. And other things, too, I wasn't sure what.

They kept me wired up, even when I was sleeping. I was wired up no matter what we were doing. They were monitoring my heart rate and my brain waves and my blood oxygen and my blood sugar and even my sperm count – that part was the most unpleasant. Anything that could be measured, Dr. Eberling was extracting and examining.

Three times a week, she had me running on a treadmill until I collapsed, sweating and gasping, followed by a full body scan in some kind of giant screeching MRI machine.

Except one day, they skipped the treadmill. Instead, Dr. Eberling did a blood-sugar test. She had me drink some thick syrupy liquid so sweet, it made me sick. I felt fizzy and dizzy and I don't know what – then, she took samples of my blood every three minutes, over and over until I finally passed out. The noise of the body-scanner woke me up.

Another day, they had me in a hyperbaric chamber, breathing pure oxygen at high pressure. That wasn't fun. I was decompressing for hours. Then, they popped me into the damn MRI chamber for another hour.

But those were the easier tests.

The worst was when they'd inject me with something that made me feel like I was drifting. I think it was sodium pentothal, or something stronger. Dr. Eberling would give me suggestions, visualizations. She'd tell me to float out of my body, float high above the world, then she'd ask me what I was seeing and feeling. She'd ask me questions, and I'd answer them like a zombie. And the whole time she was doing this, I was trapped, helpless in the shrieking MRI body-scanner.

Whatever it was she'd injected me with, I had to answer – but my answers were so jumbled and incomplete, they must have been useless. They were fragments, shards, crumbles of what I was actually experiencing. The noise of the machine was carving into me like a thousand burning needles. I couldn't escape it, I couldn't think of anything else.

The third time she did this, I almost felt like I could pop. Almost, but not quite – I could feel it clearly in here. It was a kind of orgasm. I could see it, but I couldn't reach it, I was too sedated to get aroused. Dr. Eberling asked me a lot of questions about it. She tried to push me toward it, but I couldn't get there, no matter how hard she pushed. That was the drug. She wanted me to try to pop, but she didn't want me to succeed. She wanted to identify the part of the brain that made popping possible.

Except it wasn't in the brain. It was in me. I don't know how I knew that, but I knew it. I didn't tell her that.

I didn't have the words to tell her what it felt like anyway.

I was starting to hate her.

I asked her to stop, please stop.

"We can't, Richard. We have to know. You're the best subject we've ever had."

"What happened to the others?"

"Sorry. It's strictly need-to-know."

"What are you going to do to me?"

"We're going to take good care of you. The very best care. You don't have to worry about that."

"But all the tests –"

"They're part of our research –"

"But you're hurting me."

"You're special, Richard. Very special. We need to understand your condition, how it works."

"You're torturing me. Please, let me go –"

"I'm sorry. We can't do that."

"You're not sorry at all –"

"Richard, please cooperate –"

That was when I started screaming. "I don't want to do this anymore. I want to get out of here –"

They grabbed me, wrestled me to the floor, and stabbed me with a needle.

Then, they put me on a whole other cycle of drugs.

When I wasn't sitting in a chair staring at the wall, I was lying in bed staring at the ceiling.

That lasted a week.

I had to promise Dr. Eberling that I wouldn't start screaming. What that really meant was that I wouldn't try to pop. When I finally did promise, when they finally believed me, they dialed back the daytime drugs and started another series of tests.

When they weren't testing me, I could walk around the grounds accompanied by Kent, the big black nurse. That was when I found out I wasn't being held in a hospital. It was an institute. A research place. A prison in white. It wasn't near any big cities. It was somewhere near a well-tended woodland. There was a pond, almost a lake, and there were ducks and geese on the water.

Kent was an easy-going, funny guy. He didn't talk much. He listened more than he talked. I suspect he had a recorder in his pocket. He wouldn't answer most questions. He did tell me what was going to happen to the people who had killed Tandy Jones, but not a lot more than that. I don't think he was allowed to say anything else – certainly nothing that could give me ideas. But once in a while, I did get him to admit something. I asked him once who was paying for all this, and he grunted, "Who do you think? Whose picture is on the wall?"

"The one by the entrance?"

"That's Mr. Bartlett. Mr. Brian Bartlett. The tech billionaire. But that's an old picture. He's all white-haired now."

"Why is he interested in me?"

"He's not," said Kent. "He's interested in – never mind." And that was as much as he would say.

"Come on, tell me –"

"Sorry, boy. But all that stuff is way above my pay grade. I do what they tell me, I collect my check and I go home at night, happy to have a job." He put his hand on my shoulder, as if to steady me, but he lowered his voice. "Might be the smartest thing anyone could do around here. Just keep on keeping on. And maybe, maybe it'll be okay, y'know?"

I couldn't figure Kent out. He followed Dr. Eberling's orders rigorously, but he took good care of me, too. Maybe it was me, maybe I needed to feel something, but I felt some kind of affinity –

That was the other thing.

This body had its own imperatives. Things tasted different, felt different. And that affinity? That was apparent too.

This body was gay. It was something in the brain structure, something in the chemistry, something in the entire matrix of its existence. There were visceral memories here, a physical personality. There was an internal sense of being. Desires and revulsions. Pains and pleasures.

I knew that this was something that Dr. Eberling would want to know, but I wasn't going to share it with her. I wasn't going to share anything.

I didn't trust her.

But was that the body? Or, was that me? Or, was that the life I had left behind?

If I were to pop out of here – if I could actually pop out – would I find myself inside a more trusting and loving body? Probably not. If that person was trusting and loving, that soul wouldn't be shrunken, would it? That body wouldn't be untenanted, would it?

If a soul only grows in sunlight, growing big enough to fill the body, then I would only be able to travel to dark and empty places. Places where the soul had left, or never grown, or had been beaten into remission.

I didn't tell Dr. Eberling that, either. But it was one of the reasons why I wasn't looking for an opportunity to pop. Not yet.

Not that I could. They were monitoring me so closely, every time my heart rate went up, someone came to interrupt me. I couldn't even masturbate.

Then, there were the drugs. Dr. Eberling wasn't applying a patch to me anymore. Instead, there was something in the food, or maybe it was in the water. I wasn't sure, but nothing tasted right. Maybe that was this body, too. It was like learning to drive a different kind of car. Everything was there, but it was all in different places. Unfamiliar.

But there had to be something else as well, some tranquilizer stuff. After eating, I'd feel muzzy and fuzzy and drowsy for a bit. I would sleepwalk through the next few hours. By the time it wore off, I was hungry again. When I said the water tasted funny, Dr. Eberling said it had electrolytes, she said that's what I was tasting. I didn't argue, but I didn't believe her either. I just knew that I couldn't get angry or excited. I could walk, but I couldn't run. And I couldn't pop either. That muscle of escape, that particular memory, the feeling – it was fading. It was the dulling effect of the drugs – I might never be able to access it again.

That might not be so bad. Little Richard Shields was young and healthy enough, and he wasn't the life I had fled. I could live here. I could wait and see.

Maybe. For a while anyway.

Until the night I was captured.

I wasn't there for most of it. I can't say what happened.

Usually, this body sleeps hard. Sometimes I dream, and sometimes my dreams have me untethered, floating above and away, drifting up and out of the building, over the lawns and trees, sometimes high enough to see the curve of the Earth. The darkness is broken by sparkling clusters of city lights and the first edges of dawn peeking around the distant edge of the world.

But then the body jerks, like it's been floating a foot above the bed and then suddenly falls back into the sheets and I'm yanked back into it like a dog on a leash. I wake up confused and blurry. "Huh? What?" Then after a bit of fuzzy annoyance, I sink back into a few more hours of oblivion.

On this night, I couldn't get comfortable. I couldn't get to the peaceful darkness. I drifted through the silent rooms of halfway – until I heard distant noises, like scuffling. Like rats in the walls. At first, I thought I was dreaming. There were rats in the walls where a nameless little girl lived. She was afraid of them. One of them had bitten her in the dark. So, maybe I had the memory of that still attached to me somewhere. How could I remember things without a brain to store them in? Another question for Dr. Eberling to ponder.

Then there was more scuffling and more noises, and the door to my room was opened and somebody large and dark was pressing something wet over my nose and mouth. They held it there hard. It smelled bad, like alcohol and cleanser, only worse, I couldn't breathe, and for a moment I was untethered and floating, but then I wasn't. I wasn't anywhere.

– and woke up again, all fuzzy and muzzy and confused.

I was in another place, darker and quieter.

At first, I'd thought I'd popped again.

I stared at the unfamiliar ceiling. My head was full of fog. And I could still smell a faint memory of whatever had happened in the night.

No, I was still inside the body that used to be Richard Shields. I was beginning to feel attached to Richard. I hoped the real Richard hadn't died, had just popped into a better life, one he deserved, one he had earned.

In the meantime, I would take good care of this body for him. In case he ever came back. Could poppers return to a body? I didn't know. Nobody did. Dr. Eberling didn't know. But even if Richard Shields never returned, I would be the best Richard Shields I could while I was here. A curious feeling. Empathy perhaps? Or just that the body was comfortable, like staying in a warm bed on a cold morning, while lightning and thunder raged just outside the window.

Oh, that was what I was hearing. Rain.

Rain is a light gray noise. It wraps me in a soft blanket. Outside, the world is indistinct, keeping safely away behind the pattering muffle. It's peaceful here. I drift among silent evocations of memory.

Dawn is indistinct, another shade of gloom. This time, it's a man who comes to see me. He's in his forties, I think. He wears jeans and a red flannel shirt. He's balding, gray at the temples, and wears rimless bifocals. He moves with the casual confidence of authority. Another doctor? Maybe not. He's carrying a tray. He sets it down on the table next to the bed and turns to me. "Would you like some coffee? Juice? Toast? Eggs? Bacon?"

I nod. Cautiously.

He busies himself with the tray.

"May I call you Richard?" he asks. "For convenience sake?"

I don't answer. I wait.

"My name is Karl Norton. And I promise you, nobody is going to hurt you." He puts a plate in front of me.

"Really? So why did you kidnap me?"

"We didn't kidnap you. We rescued you."

"And that's why you needed the chloroform?" I think I'm angry, I'm not sure. "That's what it was, wasn't it?"

"It was the easiest way," he admitted. "We really didn't have time to explain. You don't know why they were holding you there, do you?"

I shrugged. "They said they were studying –" I stopped. There was too much I didn't want to say. "I don't know what they were doing."

"Studying? Yes. They want to know how body-travelers do it. But first they had to capture one. So they set traps. They caught you."

"I don't know how to do it." I don't know how to ride a bicycle either. I can ride one, but I don't know how I do it. If there's an explanation, it's second-guessing.

"You're not the first one to say that. That you don't know how to do it."

"Are you a doctor?"

"No. I'm a researcher. There's a difference."

"What's the difference?"

"One discovers, the other applies." He pointed at the tray. "Eat, please."

I took a bite of toast, a swallow of juice, a piece of bacon, a sip of coffee. Next thing I knew, the plate was empty.

"I guess I was hungry."

"Are you ready to talk?"

"You talk first," I said. I wasn't ready to say much more than that.

"Fair enough." He helped himself to a piece of toast. "We know you're not Richard Shields. But we don't know who you are. We can make a guess. We've done some data-mining, but –" He shrugged. "You could be anybody. Nine hundred and thirteen possible candidates. Do you want to tell us?"

I shook my head. Richard's head. "You said you rescued me."

"That's right, we did. The Bartlett Institute for Neurological Studies, they do some serious work there – or they used to. But not any more. The real purpose of that whole installation now is the investigation of trans-migratory souls. Souls like yourself that aren't tethered to a specific body. Did they tell you why?"

"Uh-uh."

"Of course not. It's old man Bartlett. Brian Bartlett. He's terrified of dying. He has the idea that travelers are immortal. He wants to learn how to pop."

I thought about that. "Even if that means stealing someone else's body?"

"Yes. Even if that means stealing someone else's body."

"That's wrong."

"Is it? You take over other people's bodies."

"But I don't want to."

Norton shrugged. "Bartlett's a billionaire. He's used to getting everything he wants. He wants immortality."

"He won't like it."

"Why do you say that?"

"There's no control. He'll never get the body he wants."

"Interesting," said Norton.

"Are you going to keep me here too? Like them?"

Norton shook his head. "You can pop out any time you want. Or you can stay as long as you want. If you want to talk to us, we'll listen. But if you don't want to talk to us, we'll respect that, too."

"Who's 'us?' What is this place?"

"Good questions. And I'll answer them as best as I can. We don't have a name. We're just a place. We're off the grid and we intend to stay off the grid. We don't want Bartlett – or anyone else, he's not the only one – to know that we even exist. Of course, now that we've rescued you, that's not going to be as easy –"

"Am I that important?"

"To them, yes. To us…well, not so much."

"Really? Then, why did you rescue me?"

"To keep them from finding out."

"Finding out what?"

"Anything. Everything. But we'll have that conversation later. It's a long one." Norton stood then, and picked up the tray. "I think that's enough for now. If you want to rest for a while, I'll leave you alone. If you want to walk around and get a sense of this place, that's fine, too. Don't worry, you can't get lost."

He left me alone then, alone and wondering. What do these people want? What do they know? Do they know who I really am?

I was in a small room, like a cheap motel room, but one of the cleaner ones, a place of generic hospitality. I stood up unsteadily, stumbled to the bathroom and sat on the toilet, waiting until I felt steady enough to stand in the shower. There were clean clothes here, my size. Whoever Karl Norton was, whoever he was working with, they had definitely planned my rescue.

That was interesting.

I finally felt well enough to look around.

Outside, the building was low, almost sunk into the ground. The ground was rocky where it wasn't sandy. There were scrubby bushes and some low trees. A cool breeze carried a salty wet smell. A short distance away, I found a beach. It curved around, I followed it far enough to make sure.

This place – it was an island.

Another kind of trap.

I couldn't leave. Not in this body anyway.

It wasn't a large island, maybe a half-mile wide, maybe a mile in length. Large enough for long walks. There were a few hills, I climbed to the top of the highest, there were some rounded boulders arranged in a rough circle. I stood on the biggest and turned slowly. I saw ocean in all directions. Only ocean.

Below, there was a scattering of small structures hidden between two of the hills, and a couple of dug-in storm shelters. From the beach, there wouldn't be any visible structures. I didn't see a dock. I'd have to walk the whole island to be sure, but after seeing how the buildings were dug in, I got the feeling that the island was supposed to look uninhabited.

Norton found me on the hill. He brought me a peanut butter and jelly sandwich and lemonade.

"No, there's no dock," he confirmed. "We have a boat moored at the mainland. It brings in supplies once or twice a week. The mainland is that way." He pointed vaguely northeast. "About twenty miles past the horizon. Technically, we're a privately-owned ecological preserve. We're not even on most maps. As much as possible, we're invisible."

"An ecological preserve?"

"In a manner of speaking, yes. What we're preserving is us."

"You're a traveler –?"

"No, I'm not. But there are others here. You're not the only one."

"Will I meet them?"

"Maybe. We'll see." Norton explained, "This is a carefully designed sanctuary. If you ever decide to pop out, tell us – and we'll give you instructions how to contact us in your new body. An email address, a phone number, access to a small bank account, if necessary. If you want to stay in touch, you can tell us who you are and where. Or not. Your choice. If you ever want to come back – well, that depends on whether or not we can trust you. Right now, you can assume that once you leave, you won't be able to come back."

"So I'm free to go?"

Norton looked at me. "Yes, you are. But I don't recommend popping out. Not right now, anyway. You could get captured again by Bartlett's people. Or worse." He tapped my chest. Richard's chest. "Remember, this body was a trap. If you get caught again, we won't be able to rescue you. Not a second time. They know we exist now."

"What if I stay?"

"We can talk about that. When you're ready." He added, "If you stay, there are certain responsibilities."

I took a deep breath and looked around. The sun had rolled the clouds back, but there was still a patchy gray ceiling to the south. The breeze was just cool enough to keep me from feeling the heat. It was comfortable, but I decided to be skeptical. I looked back to Norton. "What kind of responsibilities?"

"That's a conversation for later. If you choose to stay."

"And if not…?"

"That's a conversation for later, too." He turned to go. "Can you find your way back?"

"I think so."

"Don't worry, it's hard to get lost here. And if you do, and you're not back for dinner, we can find you fast enough. Just don't wave down any passing sailboats."

"Are there any?"

"Probably not. But don't wave at anyone anyway."

He left me alone, sitting on a large flat rock. The sun felt good. Down the slope, the waves broke and washed across the barren sand. Except for the occasional bush, there wasn't much to see. It all looked desolate.

I needed to learn about these people. I could wait. I needed to get this body healthier anyway, build up its strength. I might be in it for a while.

Besides, the food was good here. That was something.

Crispy bacon, eggs scrambled in butter, toast spread thick with sweet strawberry jam, coffee with a hint of vanilla, I hadn't said anything to Karl Norton, I could call him Karl now, but I hadn't had food this good since –

– since before never mind.

Even a peanut butter and jelly sandwich had layers of flavor I hadn't known before.

Dinner was crisp green salad, followed by grilled fish, fresh buttered corn, and a baked potato with sour cream and chives. Dessert was chocolate ice cream. Heaven.

Yes, it was a seduction.

But it worked.

I would stay.

These people knew things. I needed to know what they knew.

My dinner companions were Karl Norton and Janet Bach. There were other people on the island, but they didn't join us. I got the sense they were deliberately keeping away.

Janet Bach was a Korean girl. Or maybe she was a woman – I couldn't tell how old she was; she could have been fifteen, she could have been thirty. She could have been nine hundred years old. She wore a dark flowing dress of no specific ethnicity. When she moved, when she spoke, she did so with a deliberate patience. She studied everything around her, especially me. It made her seem wise. Almost timeless. I pointed it out to her and she replied, "I think and I know things."

After a dinner that was so good I didn't want it to end, after coffee and ice cream and an occasional enigmatic look, she said, "Let's go look at the sunset." She took me by the hand and led me out into the evening. It wasn't a choice.

The mess hall was hidden by shallow hills and bushes, so we had to walk up a path and a few ancient wooden steps to see the sunset. The western horizon was orange, streaked with purpling clouds. The breeze smelled of salt. Janet Bach smelled of lavender.

"Um, I think I should tell you –"

"What?"

"I'm – I mean – this body is gay."

"Uh-huh, I know," she said. After a moment, she added, "I've been there."

"You're a traveler."

"I'm a raveler."

"A raveler?"

"Uh-huh."

"Broken souls need healing. So do broken places."

The distant sun touched the edge of the ocean. The western horizon became a stripe of gold. A few purple clouds shone with a glowing edge.

"Most hosts are broken," she said. "You know that, don't you?"

I considered it. "That sounds right – there's no soul in here." I tapped Richard's chest. "Nothing to heal. It died. Or it fled. I don't know."

"Yes," she said. "Yes. That's how they caught you. They kept the body alive as a trap. And you fell into it."

"But what about that little girl – Tandy Jones? She was still there, wasn't she?"

"Yes, the one you told Eberling about. That soul had gone into remission –"

"I don't think remission is the right word."

"How would you describe it?"

I thought about it. "Desperate. Hiding. Shriveled. Somewhere on the other side of despair. I don't know. I don't have a word for it, do you?"

"We say they're soul-dead. Still there, but unrecoverable."

"So what does a raveler do? You heal them?"

"We heal what we can. If we can't heal the soul, we heal the situation, the circumstances. Here's the thing, Richard. Can I call you Richard? Real healing, real recovery – that has to be self-generated." She touched my chest. "It has to come from the source within you, the real self. You."

She waited for me to react, but I was waiting to see what else she might say.

"You," she said, tapping my chest again. "You."

"What?" I said.

"Stop doing that," she said.

"Doing what?"

"You know what. Hiding. There's so much you're not saying. You're judging. You're calculating. You're withdrawing inside."

For a moment I felt fear. What was she seeing? It was probably my hesitation before every sentence. I looked at the ground, at my feet, at my hands, and finally back to her, just a quick glance. "Let's just say I'm damaged, too, and leave it at that, okay?"

"No. It's not okay. I'm a raveler, remember?"

"Please. I don't want to be coached."

"Okay." She held up her hands in a letting-go gesture. "Then maybe this conversation is over." She started to rise.

"Wait, please –"

"What?" She looked at me.

I took a breath. "You said I could be more. What did you mean?"

She shrugged. "What I just said. There's more to you than you're letting anyone know."

"Okay, um. Yes. But…think about the circumstances. People are afraid. All of us. We're born into fear. There are all the real things – like pain and rejection and abandonment – and loss, especially loss of self. But being possessed by some kind of supernatural force – that's an existential biggie. That's got to be terrifying off the scale. Wouldn't you stay silent? You don't go around telling anyone who you really are, do you?"

"If that's your conversation about it, then that's your conversation. It's not mine." She took a deep breath, studied my eyes. "Listen to me, Richard. You – the person living in that body right now – apparently, you've been through a lot. I think you desperately need to find peace. You want my help? That's what I'm here for. You don't want my help? Okay, that's fine, too. But then why are you here at all?"

"Because you people rescued me. At least, you called it a rescue."

"Were you free to leave the Bartlett Institute?"

"No."

"Are you free to leave here?"

"That's what you say. But I'm still on the island."

"The island is safe. Out there –" She pointed vaguely toward the mainland. "Maybe not. But either way, it's still your choice. What do you want? That's what you need to work on."

I took a deep breath. It hurt to breathe that deep. This body wasn't strong enough yet. "I have to stay," I said. "There are things I need to know. About everything. Maybe there are answers here. I don't know. But I need to rehabilitate this body. Meanwhile, the food is good here, better than that damn hospital – and maybe I can learn something. So what is it you want me to do and why should I do it?"

"Let me throw it back to you. What is it you want to do and why should you?"

A terrible question. One that I was not going to answer honestly. Not yet, not now, and certainly not in this life. Trust is a two-edged sword. I shook my head. "I'm not sure yet. I'm still...I'm still...whatever."

"Well, you got that part right." And then, she smiled. "You know nothing. Let's start with that." She took my hand. "Come on, it's getting dark. Let's head back. We don't have any outdoor lights. It's part of keeping a low profile."

Not just a low profile. Hidden. Nobody ever said exactly where we were, but wherever this island was, it was remote. That was fine with me. I figured we had to be less than a day's travel from the Bartlett Institute – that is, if I'd awakened the first morning after my rescue. But if they'd kept this body sedated for longer than that, a full day perhaps, then they could have transported me ten thousand miles. The island could be anywhere. I finally stopped worrying about it.

There weren't a lot of other people here, and the only real building was dug into the ground. It was irregularly shaped; bits and pieces had obviously been added onto the original structure. It was nestled between a cluster of time-rounded boulders, and most of its roof was a slope of grass and bushes. It would be invisible from the air.

I didn't meet everybody – but Janet did introduce me to Laura in charge of supplies, Wallis, who managed the kitchen, Christy, whose job wasn't clear, but I assumed it was management and security. There were others who I saw only from a distance and never got their names. I assumed they were travelers. Or ravelers.

Janet told me not to ask. "Don't go digging where you're not invited. If you want coaching, you have to ask for it. But once you ask for it, you don't get to back out when it gets uncomfortable, so if there's any rule around here, it's this one – think before you speak."

They gave me plenty of time to think.

This place – that's all anyone ever called it – had a library, not the largest, only a single wall of shelves, and not all the shelves were filled. But if I wanted a book that wasn't on the shelves, Karl could have it delivered within three days. The same was true for music and videos. The only thing that wasn't available was an internet connection. The island was deliberately air-gapped. Karl never told me how communications were managed; that was part of the security of the place.

So, there were limits. But they were understandable.

We were hiding.

From whom?

From everyone, I guessed.

There were a lot of weird stories in the world about body-poppers, a lot of fear and uncertainty in the world. Some people were blaming travelers for a lot of terrible things.

Maybe some of the stories were true, maybe most of them weren't.

"I was possessed – by an invading soul. That's who did it! Not me!"

"I didn't rape her! A body-popper got into me!"

"It's not fair to convict me. I'm innocent. I wasn't in control. A monstrous presence took over my body! It fired the gun!"

"I didn't go missing! I was kidnapped from inside!"

"I'm not gay, not really – it was a body-jumper!"

"I couldn't be pregnant! I don't know what happened those three days. Maybe I was invaded –?"

Karl said that as far as he could tell, most of those people were probably lying – it didn't matter. The damage was still done. People were afraid. And maybe that fear was justifiable. Maybe there were some seriously dangerous poppers out there. But Karl wouldn't discuss it. "It's complicated," he said.

What he meant was clear. If I wanted to learn what these people knew, I'd have to cooperate. I'd have to become one of them.

But if I didn't want to – or if I somehow failed their tests – Karl could call the mainland and have a boat pick me up. I could leave on an hour's notice. He'd even give me some money, not a lot, but enough to survive on for a while, and maybe even a new name –

I considered it.

But it wasn't a good idea. The Bartlett people were probably looking for me – well, Richard Shields. But regardless of the name, the description was probably in the system, and probably with some bad stuff attached as well, something to make sure that I would be caught and turned over. Karl said he could check on that for me – if I really wanted to go.

I walked around the island for a day or so, considering my options. Nobody stopped me. I prowled the library for a bit. I got bored and found some cleaning supplies. I dusted the shelves. Then, I swept and mopped the floors. In the afternoon, I helped unload supplies from the boat. Christy told me not to talk to anyone on the boat, so I didn't. I just did what they told me to do, carried what they handed me, put it where it was supposed to go.

Later, while lying in bed, waiting to fall asleep, I realized that hadn't been me as much as the body. Richard Shields had been a little helper. The body fell into the cleaning habit automatically. I had to laugh. The body has a mind of its own.

The next morning, I asked Janet to take a walk with me. I had some questions. She laughed. "Well, you're right on schedule." We packed some sandwiches and juice and went to the south end of the island. The view wasn't any different than the north end, it was all ocean, but there were several wave-polished rocks that served as benches.

We sat down on the widest rock and admired the clouds for a while. Finally, I said, "How does this work? What do you people know? What's the difference between the mind and the soul, and why does the body remember things, too?"

Janet took her time answering. "There's a lot we don't know," she admitted. "But here's one way to think about it. What we call a soul – that's the core. That's the part that says, 'Me!' That's the experiential kernel. It's not the mind. The mind is the conversation that surrounds and submerges the 'me.' People get confused, they think they're the mind. But that's what the mind wants them to think."

"Huh?"

"Let me try that again. The mind isn't you. It's chatter. It's opinions, justifications, rationalizations, excuses, beliefs, prejudices – it's noise. It's all the explanations that are used to define an experience. And yes, the body does have a mind, a visceral conversation of its own, made up of physical memories, pleasures, pains, impacts, satisfactions, needs, hungers – it's all the conversations the body builds around itself.

"The 'me' has a mind too – the soul, the part that experiences everything – that has its own distinct conversation of want and need and hurt and desire and hunger. It's a different conversation than the body has. It's a conversation of feelings and emotions.

"Sometimes, it's one conversation that's running things, sometimes, it's the other. Sometimes, the 'me' breaks down under the conflict between the two conversations. Who am I? Right? Am I the body? Am I the soul? Am I the performance? This is the advanced course, Richard, boiled down into three minutes. The real question – the one that nobody can answer – is where does the 'me' exist? Where is it when it's not in a body? It's not the mind-body problem, because we know what the mind is, the mind is the noise that keeps us from being the soul – no, this is the soul-body problem. How does the 'me' fit into a body? We don't know. There. Does that help?"

"Not at all."

Janet laughed. "Of course not. I told you that there's a lot we don't know. But we have a pretty good idea how it works. Mostly. And that's a start. Here's the simple explanation. Think of the body as a very complicated machine. Think of the mind as the machine's interpretations of the job it has to do. Now think of the soul – the part that says 'me' – as the operator of the whole system. Different operators can sit at the keyboard. That's us, you and I. But we also take some of the experience with us when we go to another machine."

"And that was an info-dump, right?"

"Right. That was an info-dump. Do with it what you will. Would you like a sandwich now?"

We ate in silence for a while. The day was warm, but not uncomfortable. The salt-breeze off the water felt good. "So…this raveling thing. How does that work?"

She shrugged. "Ravelers go places. We go into lives. Sometimes it's easy. Sometimes it isn't. While we're there, we try to fix the conversations that can be fixed. Sometimes we can. Sometimes we can't. But where there are things we can do, we do them."

"Are we immortal? Body-travelers, I mean."

"I don't know. Nobody does. Our best guess is no."

"Why is that?"

"Because we know that souls can be snuffed out. Ended."

"Oh." I thought about that, what it meant. "How do you know that?"

"That's a conversation for another time." She patted my hand. "It's part of the advanced course."

"The advanced course?"

"Yes, there's a whole curriculum –"

"And I'm where?"

"Pre-school," she laughed. "Look. As far as we know, you have an ability. You found it by accident. An extreme circumstance, correct? Now, do you want to turn that ability into a skill? You might be trainable. We don't know. But if you can be trained, and if you do get trained – well, it's what Karl told you. There are responsibilities. We don't train fliers. We train ravelers."

"And what if I can't be trained? Or what if I don't want to be a raveler –?"

"You have that choice, yes. But…I hope you won't choose that." There was something about the way she said it.

"Why not?"

"It's dangerous. For you. For us. But especially for you. The Bartlett Institute isn't the only one looking for travelers. And…"

"What?"

She didn't look happy. "Well, I can't go into the details – but things have happened. Bad things. That's how we know body-travelers can be killed." She said it with finality.

That was a lot to think about. I wanted to ask her for details. I needed to know. But Janet wasn't going to say any more about it. Not now, anyway. That was clear.

"Mmm," I said. She waited for me to say something more. I didn't want to say anything at all, but it was my turn to talk, so finally I asked. "What if I can't be trained. What if I…just stayed here?"

"Then, you'd be like Christy and Wallis and Laura. You'd go on staff." Janet hesitated. "They tried, they tried hard. But they couldn't get off the ground. Not reliably."

"They can't pop?"

"They can pop. But they can't control their flights. That's what we call it. Flying. And it's dangerous to keep trying if you can't control it, so they're…well, grounded. Self-grounded. And that's also why they can't go back to the mainland. It's too dangerous for anyone suspected of being a popper. So they stay here and work as staff. It's safer for them. And for everyone else, as well. We won't put anyone at risk, Richard – not anyone who can pop."

She put her hand on mine. She looked at me. Whatever she'd said before, that was preamble. This was serious. "And that's the other thing I have to tell you." She paused. "You can't take too long. You'll have to decide soon."

"Why?"

"Because you do. That's how this works." She stood up. "We can't force you. This is something you have to choose for yourself. It has to be your own commitment. Otherwise – well, otherwise, it doesn't work."

She was right about that.

I spent the rest of the day in the library. It was quiet, only shelves of silent leather-bound voices to distract me.

As near as I could tell, all of the people whose words were stored here had one thing in common. None of them had any personal experience of body-traveling. They had no evidence, only hearsay. So what they wrote was all guesswork and wishful thinking, fantasy and mythology – and a few essays of unmitigated speculation. Even the non-fiction efforts were just another kind of fiction, but without a hero, let alone a satisfying conclusion.

There were no answers here, just uninformed opinions, but a library is a good place to sit alone in silence. I could talk things out with myself – in the privacy of my own head. There was no one else I trusted.

Trust is dangerous. It's the first step in betrayal.

You can't trust anyone until you know who they are and what they want, and even then....

The irony wasn't lost on me. Janet's people didn't trust me, either.

After dinner, I asked Janet Bach if she had time to talk privately. She nodded. I followed her outside. A faint breeze smelled of salt. There were no lights out here, but the moon was almost full, and after a bit, my eyes adjusted to the night. The sky was full of stars, more than I had ever seen before. I could even make out the long veil of the Milky Way.

"All right," she said. "What do you want to say?"

"Don't you know? I mean, you must have heard it before."

"Probably, but say it anyway, Richard."

"I'm not Richard. I'll never be Richard. Or anyone else."

"So what's your point?"

"You want me to choose my next life. Okay, but I need to know what I'm choosing. Everything."

"There's really only one question. Do you want to make a difference?"

"That's not a fair question. It demands a yes answer. There's no right way to say no."

"The difference between yes and no is who you are."

"I don't want to play word games. I don't know who any of you are, I don't know what you're doing, or what you want to do – so I don't know what it is you want me to choose."

She fell silent.

She looked up at the stars for a moment, found no answer there, then sighed and looked at her hands instead. They were the only evidence of her age, with just the slightest hint of wrinkles. "This body has served me well," she said. "I like it. Your body could serve you well, too. You could build up your strength. You could go back to the mainland. You could have a new life. You could choose that. That's a choice too."

"No, it isn't. The Bartlett people are looking for me. Karl said so. You did, too. Tell me, what am I choosing instead?"

She looked at me, patience and pain in her eyes. But she didn't speak. She waited for me to go on. The silence stretched into an uncomfortable chasm.

Finally, I just blurted the rest of it. "See, here's the thing. It's not a choice unless you know what you're choosing. I haven't had a choice yet, have I? I died, but I didn't escape. I got captured into a body that was starved and beaten and too weak to cry. I escaped that one and got captured into a soul-dead body so weak and frail it couldn't stand up. I got rescued? No, I got captured again, just in a different way. Now, I'm on an island with you and Karl, and no matter how you try to sell it, the choice is still the same. Cooperate or die again. Right? Isn't that it? That's not a choice. It's just another kind of prison."

Janet Bach didn't answer, didn't interrupt. I'm not sure she could have stopped me. I had a lot to say, none of it kind. "All this talk about how everything is a choice, choose the person you want to be – you know it's a lie, but everyone says it anyway, because it's a feel-good lie. But the truth, the real truth, the hard stinking truth of it – what lies underneath all the lies? More lies. And those aren't so feel-good, are they? Because there is no choice. There never was. Choice is a lie." I stopped and waited for her to admit I was right.

Finally, she said something. "I'm sorry you feel that way."

She shouldn't have said that. It was the wrong thing to say.

"Choice is a lie!" I said it again, this time with a lot more heat. "Look around. We don't choose our circumstances. The circumstances choose us. Here you are. Here I am. So what? Did you choose this? I didn't. Did you? And yes, I do know the enlightenment speech. You don't choose circumstances, you can only choose how you respond. That's all very nice. Take a sad song and make it Buddha. But it doesn't really change anything, does it?"

I faced her directly. "Oh, wait – I could pop out, right? Maybe? I think I could, I might be able to, but if I can't control it, then what –? I just get captured again, caught in a new prison, another cage of horribles. Another empty body where the soul has fled or shriveled into a little ball of pain. Another trap of ugly circumstances, right? What kind of choice is that? You know what I want to choose? I want to be tall and beautiful and healthy and all the other good things – but that's not gonna happen, is it? Because that person – his soul, her soul, whoever – that soul is going to be so big and sparkly and overflowing with life, there won't be room in that body for me or anyone else to barge in and live. So, what's left for someone like me? All the leftovers, all the ones who didn't make it, can't make it, leaving behind a body uninhabited and uninhabitable. Am I angry? Yeah, I'm angry. I can't win, I can't break even, and I can't even get out of the game. So what's the alternative? What are you offering me –?"

I stared at her. It was an accusation as much as a demand.

She answered quietly. "The only thing I can offer you is another way to play the game."

"But I have to take your word for it, don't I? How do I know this isn't just another way to get caught? Caught in what?"

"You're right," she said.

"What?"

"I said, you're right. Most of us don't ask those questions. The ones I've worked with – they're so desperate, they'll agree to anything. You're desperate, too – but not like them. You want something else."

"What do I want?"

"You want a feeling of control. That's what we all want. That's the real choice anyway. Is the choice real – or just another limit to our options?"

"And –?"

"And...nothing." She hesitated. "I know what you're asking, but it's not my decision. See? That's another limit. And you're justified in resenting it." She stopped herself, considering her own options. "Will you wait here?"

I grunted and nodded. The air was cooling, but I wasn't uncomfortable. I had a windbreaker. I zipped it up. Janet left. She was gone long enough for me to wonder just how deep I'd stepped in it.

And why.

I knew why.

Before I died – the first time, that is – I asked questions. Too many questions.

The best that any human ever came up with is pitifully wishful. We're here to be happy, we do that by making others happy, so the purpose of life is to create joy everywhere. But if that's true, then why is there so much misery? Why was there no joy in the life I fled?

Because it's not true. It's just another feel-good lie.

The conclusion is obvious – how can there be any joy in any life I might pop into? So what choice is there?

What could Janet or anyone offer that was anything worth choosing?

When Janet came back, she was wearing a light sweater. She was still buttoning it up as she approached. "So..." she began. "I talked to Karl. He agreed."

"Agreed to what?"

"That you're an asshole," she said. "But also that you deserve to know. Come with me."

I hesitated. "What if he hadn't agreed?"

"Then you'd just be an asshole." She added, "A frustrated ignorant asshole. This way."

Janet led me around to the back of the building, to a small door I had barely noticed on the first day. I had assumed it was only for supplies and storage. But no – once inside, once past the shelves and closets, there were steps that led down to an egg-shaped space, possibly an old cave – now lined with heavy-looking dark curtains. It was a softly-lit grotto. In the center, a round table surrounded by several high-backed chairs. It looked like a place for dark, forbidden rituals. Well, of course –

She pointed to a seat, then sat next to me. "Can you get comfortable?"

I nodded. "What do you want me to do?"

"Nothing yet. Wait."

After a moment, more people came into the room, not down the stairs, but from another entrance, hidden behind the drapes. One moment we were alone, the next moment there were three other figures seating themselves. I didn't recognize any of them. One man, two women, all dressed casually – one woman wore jeans and a T-shirt, the other wore a blouse and a skirt. The man was wearing a lightweight caftan and apparently little else. The light wasn't bright enough to see details.

The woman in the jeans and T-shirt sat opposite. She looked old, but she wasn't. She said, "Right. Here's what we're going to do. You can ask questions, but every question you ask, you have to answer the same question yourself. If you try to hide anything, if you try to lie, this conversation will end immediately. Is that clear?"

"Yes."

"Tell me what you heard."

"I can ask questions – but any question I ask, I have to answer it, too. No lies. No bullshit."

"Close enough," she said. "We will have questions of our own as well. We will abide by the same rules."

"Fair enough. Who goes first?"

"You can."

"Okay. I'll start simple. Do you have names?"

"There are names attached to these bodies, yes. Or, do you wish to know the names we were assigned at birth? Or, the names we have taken since then? Which names do you want to know?"

I shrugged. "Does it matter? Am I going to need them? Am I going to see any of you again?"

"Probably not."

"Then let's not do names."

"So you don't want to speak yours?"

"That name is dead. That life is over."

There was silence from the others. I wondered if I'd said the wrong thing. But nobody moved, so I spoke first. "Um, do you want to ask me a question now?"

"When did you begin?" asked the man.

"Um, I don't know. Only a few days ago – oh, I see what you're asking. February 12, 1981." It wasn't a lie, but it wasn't the whole truth either. "And you?"

Janet answered first. "My birth body was born in April of 1897."

The woman across from me said, "August, 1843."

The woman in the blouse said, "September, 1764."

The man spoke last. "My birth body was born in July, 1567."

That startled me. "Holy shit. Really?" I stared at him. But there was nothing unusual about him, except perhaps his patient demeanor. His body was just a container. He was the oil inside the bottle.

He stared back at me. "I have been many different people – nineteen men, fourteen women. I have fought in eight wars. I have borne five children. None were body-travelers. I outlived them all. I will not bury another child. I have lived, but I am not the oldest, nor have I traveled the furthest."

"Um...how do I ask this? Do you, do any of you – do you identify as male, or female, or what?"

The woman across from me said, "More than two-thirds of all body-travelers are born into female bodies. But gender-identity often becomes irrelevant with time. How do you identify?"

"I don't know any more. I'm living in this body. I'm connected to it, I can feel it physically – but I don't feel connected. I never felt connected to my birth body either. Is that the right way to say it? Birth body?"

"Was your birth body male or female?"

I hesitated – but only for a moment. No lies, no bullshit. "Everybody said my body was male. But I felt female." That was as much as I wanted to say. I hoped it would be enough.

Apparently, it was. Nobody got up to leave.

"These are all questions that Janet could have answered." The woman studied me for a moment. "Stop wasting our time. What is it you really want to know?"

"What are ravelers? What do you do? How do you do it? Why should I join you?"

The man lifted a hand for attention. Well, he was a man right now. He could have been anything. The woman nodded to him. He faced me directly. "Ravelers are a self-chosen community. We see things from a different perspective. We have learned –" He looked to the woman, she nodded. "We have learned how to release ourselves from a body, we have learned how to insert ourselves in another body, some of us can sometimes even relocate to a body of our choosing. Most important, we have learned how to assimilate, sublimate, or if necessary even eradicate the tenant in that body."

He held up a hand to stop me from speaking.

"Yes, I know. That raises questions. But the only people who believe that tenants are bound to their bodies are tenants bound to their bodies. That's not true. You know that for yourself. But if souls are portable, then what? What does that mean? Those of us who got here before you, we've spent years, decades, centuries considering these questions. Do we have a responsibility to the world we live in? And if so, what is that responsibility? How do we apply it?"

"I think that – I mean – it seems to me –" I floundered. I wasn't sure what they wanted to hear.

"Yes. That's the conversation. I think. I mean. It seems. All of that, and more. What is our responsibility? This is an argument that started before the enlightenment, before any of us were born, and continued as an argument forever. At least until 1945, when Allied troops rolled into Germany and opened up the death camps. At that point, the argument was effectively resolved once and for all. Do you understand why?"

"Um, no. Tell me."

"It was the Hitler question. If you had a time machine, would you kill Hitler?"

"But I don't have a time machine. So the question is irrelevant."

"No. It is not. It is an essential question. Understand this. If changing one life in the past would make an enormous difference in the present, then do we or do we not have an equivalent responsibility in the present? Can we change one life today to make an enormous difference in the future?"

"The way you phrase it, there's only one answer to that question."

"So, how would you answer it?"

"It depends on the circumstances. Life isn't one-size-fits-all."

"You think so?"

"Yes. Because you're asking me to have an opinion without giving me any facts. Just theory. Give me an example."

The man paused. He looked to the woman. She said, "Suppose there's a person who has to make a difficult decision. If he decides to go to the right, some people get better, others get worse. If he goes to the left, some people get worse, others get better. One way advances science and research, the other advances the economy. Let's assume a raveler can enter that person's mind and influence that decision –"

"So you're assuming an authority over other people's choices?"

"We already answered that question."

"Yes. I heard you. Assimilate. Sublimate. Or eradicate."

She looked annoyed. "Assimilation means the raveler joins, merges, combines with the existing soul – the two become one, a new, larger entity. We do not do that often, only when a resident soul has attributes worth adding to the raveler's."

"Have you done it?"

"Yes," she said. "I have. It is not easy, but sometimes assimilation is necessary. Assimilation makes it possible for a raveler to influence a necessary or important decision."

"Does it work?"

"Not always." She sounded regretful. "Sometimes the resident soul fights assimilation. In that case, the raveler goes for sublimation or even eradication. But if the resident soul is healthy enough to resist, the result can be schizophrenia, a fragmentation of behavior. King George the Third, for example. He didn't go mad. He wasn't suffering a mental imbalance. A traveler was trying to influence his decisions –"

"You said a traveler. Not a raveler."

"We aren't the only community of portable souls."

"There are others? How many?

"That…is a different conversation, for another time."

"So there's a war going on? A hidden war?"

The woman looked to the man, nodded. He spoke quietly. "Ravelers do not always agree on goals. We are, after all, only human. Human with an additional ability. So yes, it is fair to say that there are conflicts."

"Can I ask –?"

He said, "If you look at history through a raveler's eyes, you'll see that so many inexplicable moments are suddenly clear. There are communities of ancients who wish to be kings. They started in China. The Ming Dynasty. Maybe even the dynasties before that. The Silk Road was an avenue of expansion. Some of them ended up in Egypt. And later, Rome. The Byzantine and Ottoman empires, too. Empires rise and fall, because travelers are only human – sometimes just as selfish, greedy and arrogant as anyone else. Who doesn't want to be king? But sometimes, travelers are smarter than that. Sometimes, communities cooperate, because partnership is profitable. Trade might be the most important human invention of all. How do you think science and industry and technology began? Travelers need to know how to survive and succeed. Some of that serves the needs of the species. Too much of it serves the needs of empires." He paused. "There is a joke in that, you know. All those body-bound souls who believe that the world is run by hidden conspiracies? They're not wrong, they just don't know which conspiracy. History is not what you think."

"Oh," I said. "Yes. I see. So, umm – which side are you on? You people, I mean." I looked around the room. Janet, the woman, the man, the silent others.

"That –" said the woman, "– is the right question. Finally."

"And the answer is…?" I prompted.

"What is your answer?" she said. "Remember the rules of this game? Any question you ask, you also have to answer. Which side are you on?"

"I was raised, I was taught, I had it beaten into me – life is hard, then you die. Only, that's not true, is it? Life is hard, and you don't die. You just get another life, even harder. So, if you don't die, then what is life?"

"Go on," she said.

"It's everything – that whole stupid existential question. Obviously, I'm not my past any more, so who am I? Why am I here? What am I supposed to do?"

Janet looked around and said, "See, I told you. He's right on schedule."

The woman lifted her hand from her lap, just the slightest gesture. "Shh. Let him speak."

I shook my head. I shook Richard's head. I shrugged his shoulders. "I don't know what else to say. I'm here. That's all."

"You have the ability to change your life," the woman said. "But look at the larger question. If you had the ability to change life itself, would you? And how would you change it?"

I took a breath. Richard took a breath.

I said, using his lungs, his vocal cords, his tongue, I said, "Why does life have to be hard? I'd make it easier. I'd make it so life is easy, whether you die or not. I'm tired of hard. Exhausted."

"Easy, yes. That's an interesting answer."

"You've heard it before?"

"Variations of it, yes. It's a knife that can slice many ways. Answer it again, please. Easier for whom? For yourself? Or for others? How many others? A few? Many? All?"

"For myself, first. Yes. Then – if I saw it was worth it, if I saw that others deserved it, maybe, yes, I don't know. You don't know where I came from, what happened to me, who I was or what I did. But I never learned how to be good – only hungry. You're saying that things can be different. But I never saw it."

"Do you want to tell us about that life?"

"No – that's why I haven't asked you, any of you, the same question."

"Fair enough," she said. "So answer this question instead. What do you want? What do you want to do?"

"I want life to be easy. Easier. If it can't be easy, then I want to die."

"Death is possible," she said. "But forever is a long time to go away. Let's talk about easy instead. What would that look like?"

"I don't know. Not being hungry all the time. And I don't just mean physically hungry. I mean...you know. All the other hungers."

"What are you hungriest for?"

I didn't answer. I wished she hadn't asked the question.

But she repeated the question. "This is it. The truth moment. What are you hungriest for?"

She wanted honesty. I'd give it to her. "Revenge." There. I said it.

There was silence in the room for a long moment. It felt as if they were conferring without words.

I had to say something. "May I explain that?"

"Please."

"I was hurt. A lot. It was – I don't want to talk about it, I don't want to relive it – but it was worse than you can imagine. Day after day. And I couldn't get away from it. The more I tried, the worse it got. All I could ever think about was how much I wanted to hurt back. And when I finally realized that I couldn't hurt back, that I'd never be strong enough, that I'd never have the chance, that's when I wanted to die. But even after dying, here I am, I still want to hunt them down and hurt them. I want to hurt them as bad as they hurt me. I want to hurt them worse than that. I want them to beg for mercy, so I can laugh at them the way they laughed at me. So, yeah, that's the – how did you say it, Janet? That's the conversation this soul lives in. I am an angry soul, forged in pain and anger and a rage that consumes like fire –"

I let the words pour out of me. I wanted them to hear it all, no matter what the consequences. "But I don't want to be that angry. As much as I want to escape myself, as much as I want to let go and get past all of that, as desperate as I am to find a place that's safe and easy, that's impossible for me, I'll never get there. You do understand why, don't you?"

"Go ahead. Say it...."

"This body, the one I popped into, I'm here because its conversation matches mine. It's been bullied and beaten, beaten up and beaten down. It has a visceral conversation of pain and rage. Our conversations match. They fit together. This frail little body, like the bruised little body of Tandy Jones. It calls out to a soul like me. Here, come live here, you're familiar with this. You know how to live with pain. But the irony, the horror, is that these frail little bodies are traps – it's the same cage. There's no escape. The walls are made of bone. So how can I ever fight back? Revenge remains always out of reach, always impossible."

I looked around the room, looked at each of them, Janet, the woman, the man, the other woman. All of them.

"You want me to understand that there's something else? I'd like to believe you. But I've never experienced any of the things you're talking about. Those are alien concepts to me. Words without meaning. You want me to trust you? All of you? I've never even known trust. That's another one. So I don't think there's anything any of you can say or do that will…" I didn't know how to finish that sentence, I'd run out of emotion. "…I don't know, whatever it is you want to accomplish here – with me. I am what I am."

The woman nodded, as if she understood. "Yes. Thank you. We do know something about bodies and the kinds of souls a body will attract. What you said – that's honest. Thank you for speaking so honestly. It does make a difference. Is there anything else? Anything you want to add?"

I shook the head. It felt like my head. I took a breath and shook my head. I was drained.

The woman looked around at the others. "Well then, I think we've heard enough."

"What does that mean?" I asked.

"It means we're through here."

"We're done? So…what did you decide?"

"We didn't decide anything. You did." She looked to Janet. "You can make tea now."

And with that, the woman stood up, the others did too. Only Janet Bach remained seated. She put her hand on mine to keep me in my place. "We're not done, you and I," she said softly. "Wait."

After the others had left and we were alone again, Janet faced me. "We're going to do something. I'm going to take you somewhere. Do you want to go?"

"Where?"

"It's easier to take you than to explain. Do you want to go?"

"Do I have a choice?"

"Yes."

I didn't have to think about it. I needed to know everything. "All right. Yes."

Janet reached under the table and brought up a tray with a tea kettle and a single cup. "Do you need to go to the bathroom? This is going to take awhile."

"No, I'm good."

She busied herself with the ritual of the tea. She sang words to herself while she shredded aromatic leaves into a small metal trap. She sang a different song as she lowered it into the boiling water. She sang a third song as she waved her hands through the steam, spreading the fragrance into the air. If she had said she was a witch, I would have believed her. "Breathe," she said. "Breathe deep."

I sniffed. The air had taken on a wild fragrance, almost mystical. The tea smelled of time and history. I thought of distant places – deep jungles and arid deserts, high mountains and hidden valleys. The ruins of lost cities beckoned.

At last she filled the cup. She said, "Three sips only. No more. The first sip is for the body you are living in. The second sip is for the soul that lived in this body. The third sip is for you, the soul now living in the body. Like this."

She took the cup in both hands and sipped delicately, once, twice, three times. "This is for the body. This is for the soul that lived in this body. And this is for myself."

She handed me the cup and I took my three sips. Once for the body, once for the soul, once for myself. I handed it back to her and she replaced it on the tray.

"Now relax," she said. "I want you to do as little as possible. Just sit and exist. Close your eyes. Float. Don't think. Just notice what thoughts come up. And then let them go. Let go. Let yourself float."

For the longest time, I felt nothing – just the usual noise and chatter of thoughts bubbling into existence and evaporating just as quickly. After a while, they faded into background noise. They were the rustle of leaves in the wind.

And I was floating. Drifting. Richard's body was resting peacefully where I left it. What a small frail thing. I could see each beat of its heart, waves pulsing outward from the center. I could see the white sparkle of sensations flickering along the skin, up through the arms and legs, into the spine, and finally into the glow of his brain. I was a small red smolder inside, considering all this existence.

I wasn't alone.

There were other smolders around, all colors.

I listened.

I listened hard.

Some were faint and distant, some were nearby. One was right beside –

They spoke, they sang, but not in words – only sensations, images, flickers of meaning.

It felt like a sound, like leaves rustling in a breeze, but the deeper I listened, the stronger the wind became, almost a hurricane. It pushed at me, pulled me, tumbled me –

I resisted only for a moment, then –

I let it happen.

I sang with them. I sang their tones –

And then, everything was slippery-sliding sideways, upside and down around, slicker-flickery, caught in boiling waves, adrift in the sea of souls, swimming without direction –

Here –

Who –?

Hear me –

Here –? Me?

Can you (see)(feel)(inside)(touch)(live)(be) here –?

???

(Touch) me.

Touch –

Suddenly, everything was everything and nothing at the same time, and it all made sense, each in its own way, complete and perfect, until it wasn't, wasn't anything anymore.

I woke up shivering.

I felt wrong.

Different.

Uneasy.

Sat up – more strangeness.

Feet on the floor. Where am I?

Blinked awake and looked, looked at my hands – they weren't my hands any more. They were wrinkled.

Janet's hands.

I was in her body.

Really? Is this what they had done? Is this what I had chosen?

I stood up. Nearly stumbled, almost fell. This body was weak.

Not weak.

Sick.

Something in the gut, in the bowel, in the flesh – something growing, growling, metastasizing.

Oh, you foul bitch.

All of you –

Even as I made my way to the bathroom to collapse in front of the toilet – even as I dry-heaved, great racking seizures, even as the pain rose again, exploding like magma, splattering blood into the water where it swirled and coiled like liquid snakes –

I lay on the cold tile of the floor, shivering, gasping for breath, waiting for death. My bowels and bladder emptied themselves, I lay in the stink –

All of this, everything –

As clear as the sky. Kent was their spy. He told them how the Bartlett people had caught a traveler in the nearly brain-dead body of Richard Shields.

It was never a rescue.

They wanted a body. Janet Bach needed a new one. This had all been a charade – to get me disassociated. That was why they wanted the one I'd been in. Because they couldn't know where Janet would end up if she just popped out. But Richard Shields was an option, a good one – a receptive receptacle.

They didn't need me. Didn't want me. So it was convenient to just let the Janet body die.

With me in it.

Vile creatures –

Somehow, I got myself to my hands and knees. Somehow I pulled off my nightgown. Somehow, I climbed into the bathtub and turned on the water, washed myself as well as I could. This body was shriveled and atrophied – I hadn't noticed before, Janet kept herself bundled in long skirts and sweaters. Now, naked, I could see just how withered and thin she really was.

It must have been hard to keep this body going. Swapping out must have taken whatever remaining strength it had.

The water was hot enough. I floated for the longest time. Eventually, I stopped shivering. When the water got too cold, I somehow managed to get this body out of the tub. Eventually, I found some clothes.

When I finally managed to make my way to the dining room, there was no breakfast on the table. Of course not.

There was no one here.

It didn't take me long to see what had happened. They'd abandoned me. They'd abandoned the island. They'd fled in the night.

They'd left me here to die.

I didn't have the strength – this body didn't have the strength – to be angry.

Revenge, however – I still had enough strength to want revenge. I wanted it now more than ever.

One more trap. One more prison. One more cage. Just one more bottle to pour the pain into.

Whatever noble purposes they might have believed they served as ravelers, this belied everything. This proved I was right.

I made my way to the kitchen. There wasn't much left. They'd emptied the shelves. Deliberately? It didn't matter. I found what was left of a loaf of bread. Stale. Some peanut butter, some jam. A forgotten bit of coffee. Enough for a last meal. Maybe that was evidence of mercy? Maybe they hadn't expected me to survive the night.

I ate. It helped, a little.

When I finally felt up to it, I explored. I found what had once been the communications room. The desks and shelves were empty of gear. Just a few unattached cables and wires. There was no way to call for help.

That was okay. All I needed was time. Just a little time.

I wrapped myself up in sweaters and went out to sit in the sun. I climbed the hill and sat on the flat rock where I could see most of the horizon. All I had to do was wait.

I didn't have to wait long.

There was a flicker on the horizon. It grew larger, became a boat. It looked serious. There were men standing on the bow. They had guns, but they wouldn't need them. I wasn't planning to resist.

Kent hadn't known, it was above his pay grade, but Dr. Eberling had put a tracking chip into Richard Shields' body.

They wouldn't find him here. But they'd find me and that was fine.

Janet's body must have passed out. When I came to, I was on a gurney, aboard the boat. Everything was blurry. There was something in my arm. There was an IV unit next to me. By the time my vision cleared, Dr. Eberling was hovering over me. "Do you know who you are?"

I shook my head. Janet's head.

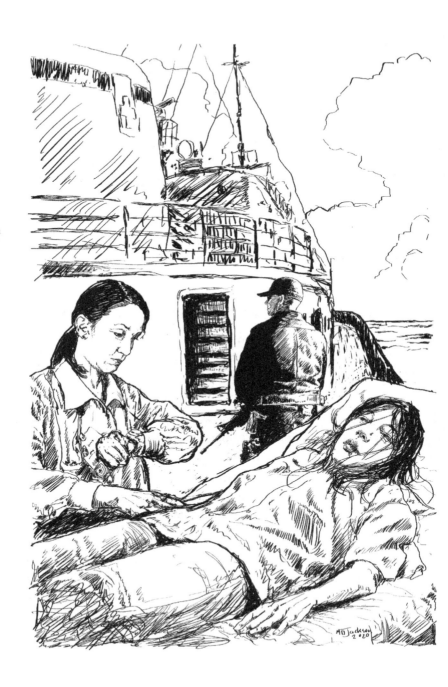

She patted my hand. "Don't worry. You're safe now. We're taking you back to the mainland."

"I'm sick," I said. "I'm dying."

"Not yet. Not for a while. Maybe not for a long time. We're going to help you."

I closed my eyes and pretended to sink back into sleep. Of course, Janet Bach hadn't bothered with treatment. It was easier to find a new host.

I'd have to wait a while – at least until I got this body's strength back up. Enough to pop. And if she died when I left, that would be okay, too. Dr. Eberling would assume it was the disease.

But I should start looking for a new host of my own immediately. Maybe one of these goons on the boat. No, too obvious.

Maybe Kent, at the Institute.

He was a simple soul. I could pop into that body easily. Eradicating the tenant wouldn't be a problem. But no, he wouldn't have the mobility I needed.

And mobility was what I needed most.

I'd gotten this far, tracking these so-called ravelers. I'd come the long way around, a lot longer than necessary, I'd submerged myself into the various identities so completely that I'd made myself invisible and unknowable even to myself. The ravelers were good – but not good enough to see how far down the rest of me was hidden. I'd been the soul they thought I was.

If they'd known who they had really brought to the island, they'd have killed the Richard body immediately – in an attempt to kill me in it.

I hadn't lied. I told them I wanted revenge.

I just didn't tell them who.

I'd been tracking them for decades. Centuries.

When they'd had me floating – when they'd been searching through my soul – I'd been searching through theirs.

I knew how to find them, now. Wherever they went. Just as there was a tracking chip hidden inside Richard Shields' body, now there was a tracking tone in every one of those souls that I'd touched.

I have never forgiven what the so-called ravelers took from me more all those centuries ago. I have hungered for revenge ever since. I have moved through a hundred different bodies in pursuit of them. I will find them, I will hunt them and I will hurt them.

This is my choice.

I will become anyone I need to be.

I could even be you.

The White Piano

Last night, I had the dream again.

I dreamt I was a child. I dreamt I was in bed, waiting to fall asleep. The walls of my room were gray and featureless, except for a black door. On the other side of the door was a long dark hall. I don't know how I knew this. The door was closed. Something was coming down the hall. When it reached the door, it started scratching to get in.

When mother went into the hospital, our grandmother came to take care of me and my sister. We were both very young. Neither of us understood why our mother had to be away for so long, but we trusted our grandmother. She fed us, bathed us, and tucked us in every night. She kissed us and stroked our heads and told us that Mama was getting better and would be home soon, we just had to be patient a little longer.

Then she'd tell us a bedtime story, a different tale every night. She never read from a book. She only told us true stories.

One day, Grandma got a phone call that made her very sad. When we asked her what was the matter, she didn't want to say. But finally, she gathered us in her arms and told us that Mama would not be coming home after all. She had not gotten better in the hospital, and this morning, she had passed away.

"Did she go to Heaven?" we asked.

Grandma hugged us close and said, "Nobody knows where you go after you die, because nobody has ever come back to tell us. No matter what anyone says, nobody knows. That's why it's so scary. We don't like not knowing." Grandma was not very religious. She said that a loving God would not have allowed so much evil and cruelty to happen in the world, so she was going to take her business elsewhere, to a better class of deity. But she never told us who that was.

That day, however, we didn't care about God. We all hurt too much, and we cried and cried for a very long time. I didn't even know why I cried so much. I hadn't seen my mother in so many months that she had turned into a memory of a different time. I had learned to live without her. But I cried just the same. Finally, we all climbed into bed together and just held onto each other until we fell asleep.

In the middle of the night, I thought I heard a scratching in the wall. I mentioned it to Grandma the next morning. She said it must have been a mouse. The house was very old and every winter, there were always a few mice looking for warmth. This was the first winter without a cat; we had not yet replaced Winston, maybe we should do that soon, so it must have been a mouse.

We slept with Grandma for another two nights before she made us go back to our own beds. She laughed and said, "You two snore too loudly." But it was really Grandma who snored. She sounded like a great grumbly bear hibernating in a deep dark cave. When I said that to Emma we both laughed.

And then when Emma told Grandma what I'd said, Grandma made a squinched-up scary face and growled horribly at us. Then she chased us around the bedroom insisting she was going to eat us all up, while we shrieked and laughed and ran back and forth around the bed, until finally we scrambled underneath it, thinking we'd be safe. But no – she crawled under the bed with us and gathered us into her arms, and we all had another long cry.

I didn't want to go back to my own bed, but Grandma put me into one of her big flannel nightgowns and said that would be just the same as her holding me close all night long. It wasn't the first time she'd popped me into a nightgown; sometimes my pajamas were still in the laundry or hadn't come out of the wash on time, but tonight was different. She said this was Grandma-magic, she'd put a blessing on the nightgown and it would keep me safe all night long.

It was a strange feeling not wearing pajamas, not having that band around my waist, my legs feeling free and naked. I wasn't uncomfortable, but I wasn't ready to fall asleep either. I was confused and my head was full of churning thoughts.

That's when I heard the scratching again.

I listened as carefully as I could, but it didn't sound like a mouse, not to me. It sounded familiar, but I couldn't place the memory. It was like one of those bits of melody that pops up in your head – you know you know it, but you don't know where it came from. It sounded close, like just outside my room, but then after a while, it went away.

In the morning, Grandma asked me how I slept. I told her okay. She frowned and squinted at me. "Didn't my nightgown keep you safe and warm?"

I said the nightgown was okay. It was nice and soft. But I heard scratching again.

Grandma made a face. "I didn't hear anything." She thought about it. "Maybe it was the branches from the big tree rattling against that side of the house. It must have gotten windy. I'll bet that's what you heard. I'll have Mr. Lopez come out and trim them back."

"It didn't sound like branches to me."

"What did it sound like?"

"I don't know. It just didn't sound like branches. It sounded like something scraping. Like scrubbing a pot. Or maybe sharpening a knife."

"Well," she said. "Yes. I suppose it could sound like that. I'll call Mr. Lopez after breakfast."

Mr. Lopez came out that afternoon. Emma and I stood a safe distance away and watched him as he climbed his ladder and cut off branches with a chainsaw. The limbs of the tree fell crashing to the ground, raising little clouds of dust and dry autumn leaves. After a bit, he climbed down from the ladder and cut the branches into smaller pieces. He loaded everything into the back of his truck, and put an envelope into Grandma's mailbox, his bill.

It was getting dark when he finally drove away. Clouds were piling up in the distance. The air smelled cold and damp, but not like rain. Grandma said it wasn't ready to be a real storm yet.

That night, when it was time to get ready for bed, I started to reach for my pajamas, then changed my mind. I looked at Grandma's nightgown and frowned. No. It wasn't Grandma's nightgown that would make me feel safe.

I walked down the hall to Mama's room. Nobody else was around, but I closed the door behind me anyway. Mama's nightgowns were all in the top drawer of her dresser. Feeling like a thief, I sorted through them until I found the one I wanted. It was very light, very pale and silky-smooth. It was almost blue, but not quite, and if you looked carefully, there were tiny flowers printed into the material.

I took it out of the drawer reverently, like something sacred. I put it on top of the dresser and gently closed the drawer. Biting my lip, I looked at Mama's nightgown for the longest time. Finally, I reached out and stroked it with my fingertips. I'd never felt anything so soft. A minute longer and I gave in to temptation. I picked it up and held it to my nose. It smelled like Mama. I hadn't realized how much I'd missed her until just this moment. I buried myself in the faint smell of her perfume.

I wasn't planning to put it on, or maybe I was. I told myself I just wanted to keep it next to me because it still smelled like Mama. But once in my room, I wondered what it would feel like to wear it, to feel this incredible smoothness against my naked skin. Mama wouldn't mind, I knew. It would be like having her hug me all night. And that would be better than Grandma.

I told myself I shouldn't, but then I told myself that if I didn't, I'd always be left wondering what it felt like, what I'd missed, so finally I took off all my clothes and pulled on Mama's nightgown. It was almost too big for me, hanging down to my feet, the sleeves falling past my hands, I didn't care.

Feeling daring, I turned and looked at myself in the full-length mirror – it made me feel confused, wicked, embarrassed, ashamed, and delicious, all at once. I stood there for I don't know how long, until all the different feelings became too much.

Then quickly, before anyone could see, I jumped into bed and snuggled under the covers feeling very special, maybe even a little rebellious. For a moment, I didn't move at all, then finally I let myself feel the softness of the material, stroking it against my chest and belly and legs and everywhere and feeling oh so very luxurious – but also feeling sad and strange and close to tears, wrapped in the sweet smell of my lost mother.

About the time I started to drift off, I heard the noise again. Something scratching. I rolled up on one elbow and listened. I wondered if I should get out of bed and go look. It sounded like someone scraping something hard off of old linoleum. Or maybe someone sharpening a knife on a grinding wheel. Or maybe –

There was a story I'd read once. Downstairs, we had a room filled with wonderful old books and I was allowed to read any book I wanted, but only if I showed it first to Mama or Grandma and asked for permission. Mostly, I did, but sometimes I didn't. One of the books was a collection of stories by Edgar Allan Poe. It was called *Tales of Mystery and Imagination*. Grandma said I wasn't old enough to read it yet, so I only read it when she was out of the house and wouldn't catch me.

One of the stories was about a man whose hearing was so intense, he could hear the sounds coming from the chambers beneath the house, where his sister was scratching at the lid of her coffin, frantically trying to get out.

I wondered if that was the noise I was hearing.

Maybe Mama hadn't really died. Maybe Grandma was lying to us. Maybe she was in a box underneath the house, screaming and scratching in desperate frenzy.

The more I thought about it, the more certain I became that the noise was coming from the basement. Forgetting what I was wearing, I crept out of bed. I almost tripped on the hem of my nightgown,

Mama's nightgown, then grabbed the front to hold it up. I crossed to the door and peeked out of my room. The whole house was so dark, it must have been past midnight. Only the vaguest hint of illumination outlined the hall.

I listened for the scratching again.

I stepped into the hall, started cautiously toward the stairs – then caught a glimpse of something pale moving at the far end of the corridor, something ghostly. I yeeped and ran back to my room, slamming the door in fright – until I remembered there was a full-length mirror at the end of the hall and I'd seen my own reflection. I'd seen Mama's nightgown. I would have laughed out loud if my heart hadn't been pounding so hard.

When I caught my breath again, I counted to ten, then I counted to ten again just to be sure, then I opened the door of my room, very very slowly, so slowly it creaked, and finally finally, even more slowly than I had opened the door, I peeked around the heavy wooden frame to look down the hall.

There was nothing there.

Of course there wasn't.

Maybe just the slightest hint of a face, a distant pink blur.

I waved my arm and something in the distance waved back.

Bravely, I stepped out into the hall and so did my reflection. I waved my arms first away from my sides like an animated Jesus, then over my head like a victory cheer. So did my reflection. Again. And again. I giggled.

I held out the sides of my nightgown and waved them like wings. A distant angel waved back. A minute more and I was twirling and dancing, capering with my faraway twin, feeling deliciously free and dangerous.

I pretended I had a twin brother dancing and giggling with me, someone who knew and shared everything without my ever having to say a word, someone who was my other half so complete that I would never have to feel alone again, someone who liked me completely because we were both the same. He was another me.

So, I danced with my ghostly brother down the hall until – abruptly, I heard a sound that wasn't me and I dashed back into my room and carefully closed the door. After a minute, I peeked out again.

There was no one in the hall.

Except –

Down at the far end of the hall, even beyond that – in the faraway dark distant reflection in the mirror, something pale and soft still fluttered and twirled and danced. It looked like a woman.

She waved to me.

I ran back into my room, nearly tripping in the nightgown, pulling it off as fast as I could and flinging it aside – **it was haunted!** – I scrambled naked into bed, pulled the covers up over my head, wrapped myself tight in the blankets, and then shrieked and sobbed into my pillow, shaking and trembling in terror so intense I thought I was going to die.

I must have fallen asleep sometime. The next thing I knew, the morning sun was screaming in through my bedroom window. Not streaming, screaming. That's how I experienced it – a howl of angry dawn. I was so snarled in my sheets I couldn't move. I had to roll out of bed and onto the floor with an ugly thump, pushing and kicking at the shroudlike embrace. I felt like a mummy.

Somehow I twisted free and leapt backward away from the tangled mess as if I had escaped from the jaws of some hideous beast. Standing there naked, I remembered what had happened the night before. I saw Mama's nightgown on the floor, and Grandma's too. I picked them both up and shoved them quickly into a bottom drawer, embarrassed.

I grabbed some clothes from the closet and pulled them on hastily. I was confused and exhausted and feverish; I knew I had to get out of the house immediately. I had to get away as far as I could.

Cautiously, I opened the door, I peeked down the hall. Bars of light slanted across the corridor from the open window at the end. The soft yellow daylight revealed everything. The noise I'd heard, the one that startled me – that was the wind blowing an unlocked window open, the tall one that led out onto what Grandma called "the widow's walk," a second story porch that wrapped around the old house. Grandma called it an architectural horror, I thought it was a great place for watching the world. The window had swung inward, lifting the light summer curtain – it was still blowing across the mirror, fluttering and dancing. And waving.

That was what I'd seen. Nothing more.

I rushed the last few steps to the window and pulled the curtain away from it and shut the window as quickly as I could and locked it firmly. The curtain fell back into place, once again shading the light and muting the bars of drifting dust-motes. The hall was safe again.

But I didn't feel relieved. No. Something had caused the window to open when it did. That's how these things worked. I'd read enough ghost stories by then to know. Whatever supernatural thing happens, it has to look like a natural event. That way, only the believers will see what's really happening. The ones who don't believe – they're the ones who always get caught unawares and unprepared.

I wondered if I had caused it – if by putting on Mama's nightgown, I had somehow angered her. I didn't want Mama to be mad at me.

After breakfast, after Emma went outside to look for autumn leaves to press into her scrapbook. I stayed with Grandma at the breakfast table while she finished her tea. I asked her if there were such things as ghosts.

She put her teacup down and looked at me, "Did something happen last night?"

"I thought I saw a ghost." I didn't tell her about putting on Mama's nightgown, but I did tell her about the scratching I heard and what I saw when I opened my door. "I looked down the hall and saw something waving at me. I thought it was Mama – Mama's ghost."

Grandma didn't say anything. She poured herself another cup of tea. "Lots of things happen in the world we can't explain.
"That's why there are scientists. It's their job to look for explanations. Did you find one?"

I told her how the window had blown open in the night, letting the curtain flap in front of the window.

"There, you see."

She waited for me to agree.

I didn't answer. I just bit my lip and stared at my hands in my lap.

"What?" She didn't say it loudly, she didn't have to, it was still a command. "Tell me, sweetheart."

When I still didn't answer, she reached over and patted my arm. "All right. You don't have to if you don't want to. If you change your mind –"

"Grandma," I blurted, "I think Mama's mad at me. I think she blew the window open on purpose."

"Now, why on Earth would your mother be angry with you? She loved you very much. More than you know. All she wanted was to come home and be with you and Emma." I noticed that she didn't tell me there were no such things as ghosts, that Mama couldn't have been there in the hall, couldn't have opened the window.

I balled up my hands into fists and held them against my belly. Tears ran down my cheeks as I admitted, "I took her nightgown out of the drawer. It smelled so much like her, I wanted to wear it and sleep in it, so she could have her arms around me like you did. But I think Mama's mad at me for taking it, for putting it on, for everything. I'm so sorry, Grandma –"

All these years later, I can see that my grandmother was a very pragmatic woman, and a very loving one too. She didn't care about the nightgown. All she saw was a little boy blubbering in distress. She pulled me to her and held me close, and let me sob into the huge pillows of her bosom. I can still remember how safe I felt in her arms.

"Sweetheart," she said, "you go ahead and keep your mother's nightgown. You go ahead and wear it whenever you want to feel close to her. I'm sure that's what she would have wanted. I know it's what I'd want if you needed to feel close to me."

I sniffed hard and looked up at her. "Really?"

"Really," she said.

"But what about the ghost?"

"Ahh, yes. What about the ghost? Well, you let me think about that for a bit, okay?"

"Okay."

We sat there in the kitchen for a while, talking about nothing in particular. Grandma stroked my hair, she said I had such beautiful hair it made her jealous. She asked me which nightgown I'd taken. I told her the really soft one, the blue one. She said that was a good choice, that's the one she would have chosen too, and that's when I realized it really was all right with her.

After a while, Emma came back in, carrying two huge red leaves she'd found in the back yard. When she saw me in Grandma's lap, she put them carefully down on the kitchen table and announced, "My turn now." I slipped out of Grandma's hug and Emma climbed up onto her lap with a happy expression.

"Was he crying?" she asked.

"No, course not," Grandma said. "But it would have been all right if he did. Boys can cry too."

"Oh, okay." And then she buried her face against Grandma's neck. After a minute, she pulled back and looked into Grandma's face. "When I grow up, I want to have big shaky bosoms like you. They're nice and warm."

Grandma laughed at that, we all did, and we kept laughing about it all the rest of the day. Every time Emma wanted to make us giggle, all she had to say was, "I'm going to have big shaky bosoms too."

Even funnier was when I said it and Emma frowned at me and said, "You won't have any place to put them," and I snapped right back, "I'll put them on my girlfriend." That made Grandma howl with laughter. I wasn't sure why that was funny – whether it was the big shaky bosoms or the idea that I might someday have a girlfriend. I didn't know.

After dinner, after our lessons, after our practice at the piano (and after Grandma showed us how that part of the concerto should really sound), after our cocoa and biscuits, it was time for story and bed.

Grandma said we should each put on our favorite nightgown, she looked directly at me when she said it, so I knew what she meant. She was saying it was all right, and we'd all snuggle up together for a very special story.

I went to my room and dug out Mama's nightgown. I put it on slowly, then made my way back down the hall to Grandma's room, knowing it was all right, but embarrassed anyway. When I came in, Emma looked at me and screwed up her face in confusion. Finally, she said, "Isn't that Mama's –?" But Grandma said, "Shh, honey. It's his now. Mama wanted him to have it, so she could hug him all night long, even when she's not here. Now, come snuggle up with me."

We both got into bed with her, one on each side, and Grandma wrapped her arms around us, pulling us close. "I am going to tell you a story that I have never told anybody before. It's a true story, and it happened to me when I was your age." I wasn't sure if she meant me or Emma, I didn't ask. Maybe she meant it that way for each of us.

"It's a very long story and it's very complicated, so you'll have to pay close attention. But if there's anything you don't understand, you just ask, and I'll explain as I go."

There's a hotel in New York, Grandma said, called The Algonquin. It's very famous.

Grandma said she stayed there once when she visited the city. It was her honeymoon. She said it was a very nice hotel, but all she remembered was that it felt old and dark and dusty.

But in the twenties, the Algonquin was a place where a cluster of self-indulgent writers and actors would gather for lunch and repartee every day. Some of them were columnists, and whenever they had nothing important to say, they wrote about each other. They called their gatherings The Algonquin Round Table.

This made them famous for being famous.

The most famous was a lady named Dorothy Parker, but the circle included Robert Benchley, George S. Kaufman, Heywood Broun, Harold Ross, and Alexander Woollcott. Sometimes people like Tallulah Bankhead, Edna Ferber, Estelle Winwood, and Harpo Marx would join them. I don't know if Harpo said much though.

Grandma said that there were even more important gatherings of writers and artists in Europe. She mentioned several cities, but I remember only Berlin and Paris.

The Paris salon, she said, was started by Gertrude Stein. It included F. Scott Fitzgerald, Sinclair Lewis, Thornton Wilder, Ezra Pound, Georges Braque, Henri Rousseau, Henri Matisse, Pablo Picasso, James Joyce, and of course, Alice B. Toklas. Although they didn't meet as regularly, they also had a favorite gathering place, a bistro on the left bank of the river Seine.

While Ernest Hemingway was still a struggling author, he would show up to cadge drinks and meals from the others, but very quickly he established himself as an efficient reporter, and even demonstrated some skill with short stories. Occasionally, publishers dropped by. Sometimes, they paid for meals. Sometimes they even bought the writers' stories.

"Did you know Hemingway?" I asked.

"No, I did not," Grandma said, "but I almost knew his German publisher. I lived in his house for a while. He'd made a lot of money printing German translations of Hemingway and other authors."

It was the twenties, and even if they didn't know it then, it was a marvelous time to be alive. It was the first generation with radios and telephones and automobiles and record players. There was music everywhere. People were discovering a different way of life.

But it was also the first decade after the Great War, and it was a terrible time for Europe. A whole generation of young men had died in the trenches, and even though no one really knew how to explain what they were all feeling, there was a terrible emptiness everywhere. So they tried to cover it up with wild parties, drinking and dancing and lots of casual sex, instead of learning how to fall in love.

Germany had lost the war, so the German government was forced to sign a peace treaty at Versailles. Germany couldn't build any more warships or guns and they had to pay the Allies for the cost of the war, billions of dollars. This impoverished the country, leaving almost no money for anything else.

The Nazi Party blamed the economic turmoil on the Jews. They blamed the Jews for starting the war. Although the Nazi Party had begun as an extremist movement, by the end of the decade it had won nearly a third of the seats in the Reichstag.

Fearing darker times ahead, some of Germany's Jews began emigrating, quietly making their way westward. Some ended up in Paris, others passed through on their way to America or other places.

After Hitler became *Führer*, the trickle of refugees grew rapidly. Some sold off as much of their goods and property as they could. Others, those who could afford it, brought their art and furniture with them. One of these was one of the publishers who had often bought drinks for the Paris group. He had been very successful all over Europe, so he was a very wealthy man. He had translated and published many of the writers in the Paris group so he was welcomed into their ranks. His wife owned a beautiful white piano, and they brought it with them to Paris at great expense. The piano had been his gift to her when they married.

The publisher's wife had been a famous concert pianist, almost a prodigy. Before the Great War, she had played concerts all over Europe – Vienna, Paris, Berlin, all the major capitals. Audiences marveled not only at her sublime technical skills, but were also deeply moved by the emotional depth of her performances.

As the story goes, on their wedding night, instead of taking her to bed, her new husband took her to the room in his house that had previously been his private study, but unknown to her, he had ordered it remodeled into a special room just for her, a music room, and in it he'd installed the most beautiful grand piano she had ever seen, all gleaming white with exquisite gold trim. It had been designed and built for an extravagant movie musical, but the movie was never filmed because the writer and director had left Germany for America.

The publisher's new wife sat down at the keyboard and began to play for him. She played her favorite piano pieces – Beethoven and Mozart and Liszt. He sat and listened, enraptured. She played for hours and they did not go to bed until dawn finally lit up the curtains with the pink light of morning. It was, they both said, the most romantic wedding night in the world.

By the middle of the thirties, it was apparent that a reinvigorated Germany was preparing for war again. There was a civil war in Spain, and German weapons were being used to crush the anti-Franco factions. Among the members of the Paris Salon, there was a gloomy awareness that this was a preview of Germany's renewed military strength. Pablo Picasso painted a terrifying mural called *Guernica*, to portray the horror of a Spanish town subjected to aerial bombing by Germany's Nazi Luftwaffe.

With all this talk of a new war, Paris didn't feel safe anymore, so the publisher and his wife retreated again, this time to England. Of course, they brought the piano with them, again at great expense. They bought a small estate near Durham and installed the white piano in a spacious parlor. But the wife died of pneumonia that first winter, and the husband covered the piano with a heavy sheet, locked up the parlor, and never went in there again.

Later, when the Nazis began bombing London, thousands of children were evacuated and sent to live in the country. Even so, one in ten people killed in the Blitz were children, not all of them were as lucky as Grandma.

Grandma and her younger brother and sister were sent to live in the publisher's house, a small manor not too far from the Scottish border. The publisher was off in some place called Bletchley, working for the British government as a translator, so the house stood empty except for a small caretaker staff.

For whatever reasons, Grandma was never sure why, she and her two siblings were the only children boarded in that house. The two younger ones were safely established in an upstairs nursery, but Grandma was put in an unused room downstairs. It was a large L-shaped room at the southwest corner of the house. Other than her bed and a chair, all the other furniture in the room was draped with sheets.

Charlotte-the-housemaid showed her where to unpack. She was a big red-haired Irish lady who had no children of her own, never having found a man big enough to sweep her off her feet, or so she said. Consequently, she was delighted to finally have some children to take care of, especially ones old enough to be out of diapers.

"I'll have to get you some sheets and towels," she said, and hurried off to find them. Grandma hadn't even put down her suitcase yet, everything was happening so fast. She dropped it on the rug and turned around, staring. She couldn't help herself. The walls were almost all bookshelves, except for several old portraits of men and women. The men were all standing sternly, the women all sitting politely. That made Grandma laugh.

Around the corner was a huge piano-shape covered with a large white sheet. Curious, Grandma lifted up the edge of the sheet to peek. As soon as she saw it was a grand piano, she cried out with delight and clapped her hands. Quickly, she pulled the sheet off and let it fall to the floor forgotten, amazed at what she saw.

No longer gleaming, the fabulous piano had turned a faded gray. The damp air of northern England had not been kind to it. The beautiful instrument's once-glamorous paint was now streaked with deep cracks, even peeling away at the edges, but in the gloomy afternoon light, it looked magically silver to Grandma. It was an enchanted fairy piano, wonderful and mysterious.

Carefully, she walked around it, touching it gently with her fingertips, tracing the gold trim. When she got to the front, she opened the fallboard and let her fingers stray across the yellowing ivory keys. They felt as smooth and seductive as if they were made out of silk. Grandma couldn't help herself. She started playing "Für Elise," which Ludwig Van Beethoven had written for a little girl named Elise. All these years later, nobody is sure who Elise really was. It's still something to argue about.

"Für Elise" is easy to play, and almost every beginning piano student learns it sometime – that and "Twinkle, Twinkle, Little Star," which started as a nursery rhyme, but ended up being part of Haydn's "Surprise" symphony. Mozart wrote some variations on it too.

But Grandma didn't get very far into the piece before Charlotte-the-housemaid came running in, red-faced and shouting, "Oh, no, no, no!" She closed the fallboard, almost slamming it down on Grandma's fingers. "You must never play this piano," she said. "Never." She started gathering up the sheet from the floor.

"Why not?" Grandma asked.

"Because you mustn't. It's forbidden," Charlotte-the-housemaid said, clutching the sheet to her chest. "This piano belonged to the Missus. It was her favorite thing in the whole world. She used to sit in here and play for hours, the most beautiful music you ever heard. But then she took sick suddenly and died, and the Mister ordered that no one should ever play this piano again, because it was hers."

"But it's such a beautiful piano. And I know how to play the piano. I used to practice every day. It isn't fair that it's here and I can't play it. I like playing the piano. I need to practice my lessons."

That's when Charlotte-the-housemaid said, "If it were up to me, I wouldn't mind. But…" She lowered her voice, "…You don't want to make the ghost angry, do you?"

"Is there really a ghost?" Grandma asked.

Charlotte-the-housemaid had come from a large family in Dublin. She had helped raise two little sisters, so she was very good with children. Now she lowered her voice even more, down to the quietest whisper – she looked around in all directions, very conspiratorially, and said, "Now, I'll tell you, sweetie, I don't believe in ghosts, but I think maybe the Mister does, because every few months a man comes up from town just to tune the piano, even though no one's allowed to play it, so maybe the Mister wants to keep the ghost happy – what do you think?"

"I think it's not fair," Grandma announced. "I want to play the piano." Grandma was always very stubborn, even as a little girl. She said she once out-stubborned a cat, but that might have been another of her stories. But this time, however, she sat on the bench and folded her arms – and stuck out her lower lip. And that was always a sign of trouble. Emma does it too.

It must have worked because Charlotte-the-housemaid said, "Now, sweetheart, you know I'm not supposed to go against Mister's instructions." Then she took a big deep breath and added, "But he's not here and you're right, it is a perfectly good piano, and maybe what he don't know won't hurt him, will it?" She sat down next to Grandma on the bench and opened the lid for her. "Maybe a little bit, just for right now?"

So Grandma started to play her favorite piece. She didn't need the music. She knew it by heart. She played it every time she sat down at a piano. It was called "The Aquarium" and it was written by a Frenchman named Camille Saint-Saëns. It's part of a larger suite called *The Carnival of the Animals*. There are thirteen other parts, each one dedicated to a different animal – elephants, asses, swans, kangaroos, hens and roosters, tortoises, and even pianists who I guess are some special kind of animal too. But Grandma's favorite part was "The Aquarium."

If you close your eyes, you can almost see the fish moving through the rippling water, drifting above the rocks, nibbling and bubbling, lurking beneath lily pads, and looking back at you with black lidless eyes. Fish don't blink. That always makes me wonder what they're thinking. Do fish even think?

When Grandma is in an angry mood, she plays Beethoven, usually the *Pathetique* sonata, which is much harder and has lots of ferocious pounding. She says that's how she works out her upset, but Emma and I think it's how she warns everyone to leave her alone for a while.

But this time, this night – back when she was little – sitting at the keyboard of that strange and wonderful piano, she played "The Aquarium," and sitting there next to her, just listening, Charlotte-the-housemaid started weeping.

Grandma stopped, frightened and concerned, but Charlotte-the-housemaid touched her arm and said, "No, no, honey. Keep playing. Keep playing." She took out her handkerchief and wiped at her eyes while Grandma played through the piece. When she finished, Charlotte whispered, "Again, please." And then once more after that as well. Grandma played "The Aquarium" three times before Charlotte-the-housemaid gasped, as if in pain, and said, "No more. No more for now." She reached over and closed the fallboard.

"That's my favorite piece," said Grandma.

"It was her favorite too," Charlotte-the-housemaid said. "She used to play it all the time." She nodded to the portraits of the lady. There were two.

The portrait on the left showed her as a beautiful young woman, her hair piled high on top of her head in the style of the time. All dressed in white with just a bit of neck and bosom revealed, she sat quietly in front of the piano, hands resting primly in her lap. Her smile had an impish quality and according to Grandma, you could almost see the twinkle in her eyes.

The portrait on the right showed her as she was the year before she died, thicker around the waist, hair all white now to match the dress, a different dress, much more prim, a higher lace collar around her throat, but the same pose of course, sitting in front of the piano with her hands held quietly in her lap. The smile was older, kinder, less mischievous, but the twinkle in her eyes was still there – if you looked for it.

"She was so beautiful," Grandma said.

"Yes, she was. The Mister loved her very much. We all did. She was kind to everyone. And always laughing. Always so happy." Charlotte-the-housemaid stroked the top of the fallboard. "Never a day went by that she didn't come in here and play, sometimes for hours and hours. The house was filled with music always. You could hear it everywhere, even to the farthest corners of the second floor, and even down in the pantry, everywhere."

"She must have been very good."

"Oh, she was. Very very good. She said it was because she practiced every day. She had to if she was going to play for kings and queens. The Mister once invited her to take a walk in the garden – it was such a beautiful day – but she said she needed to practice. He said that nobody would hear the difference if she skipped a day, but she just smiled at him and said, 'I would hear it.' That's how good she was."

"I'd like to be that good," Grandma said.

"You'd have to practice every day," said Charlotte-the-housemaid.

"Could I?" Grandma asked.

Charlotte-the-housemaid stared at the two portraits on the wall, first one, then the other. Finally, she patted Grandma's hand. "I miss the music. We all do. I guess it would be nice to have a little music here again."

"But won't the ghost get angry?"

"Only if you miss a note or play it wrong," said Charlotte-the-housemaid sadly. "That was the only time I ever heard her say a cross word – that was toward the end, when her hands weren't working right anymore. Hush, no more questions now. It's time for you to go to bed."

The music room bent around the southwest corner of the house. Grandma's bed was in one leg of the L, the piano was in the other, so Grandma couldn't see it around the corner, but she said it was nice to know it was there. She was so excited to have a piano again, she couldn't sleep. She could hardly wait for morning. There were huge stacks of music piled up on the shelves behind the piano. She wanted to sort through all of them. Maybe staying here in Durham wouldn't be so bad after all.

Grandma said she fell asleep imagining a great big concert hall, and a silver piano in front of a thousand people, all the women so beautiful in evening gowns, all the men so handsome in shiny black suits, and she was on stage, all in white like the lady in the paintings, and of course she was playing her favorite piece, "The Aquarium" by Monsieur Camille Saint-Saëns. She could hear it as clearly as if she were actually there in the hall.

In the morning, the whole household gathered for breakfast. Grandma said the kitchen was enormous. There was a huge wooden table in the middle of it where Cook pounded out the dough for the day's bread or carved slices off a big ham. The table was surrounded by tall wooden chairs for the kitchen staff and hanging over everything and everywhere, to hear Grandma tell it, were all kinds of pots and pans, cutlery and sieves and spoons and stirrers, anything that Cook might need to grab in a hurry.

The far wall of the kitchen was a giant fireplace, deep enough to walk into, and wide enough that if you wanted to serve roast herd, you could lay the fire for it here and still have room left over for wild boar on a spit.

But today, there were only fried eggs and sausages, toast and jam, but no butter. The only reason they had eggs, there was a coop with six chickens in back of the house. Grandma said Cook was very unhappy about having three children in the house, not because she didn't like cooking for children, but because if the children all had eggs for breakfast, there wouldn't be any for staff, including her. But Charlotte-the-housemaid told Cook to hush up with her complaints. She poked Cook's overstuffed waist and said, "Besides, you've already had enough eggs in your life." Cook waved a huge wooden spoon at her, as if it was a club, but then grumbled away to stir the porridge.

As soon as Cook's back was turned Charlotte-the-housemaid turned to Grandma with a stern look on her face. She lowered her voice and said, "You mustn't play the piano in the middle of the night anymore. You'll wake everybody up."

That confused Grandma. She said, "I didn't. I was in bed all night long."

Charlotte-the-housemaid frowned and said, "Don't you tell me no lies, Missy, or we'll not be getting along very well."

That made Grandma cry and she ran from the kitchen in tears. "I'm not lying, I'm not!" She went to her big L-shaped room and threw herself on her new bed, sobbing. That was where Charlotte-the-housemaid found her.

"Now stop that crying this minute. I won't have it, you hear me?"

Grandma sat up stubbornly and glowered at Charlotte-the-housemaid the way only a little girl can glower. "I didn't lie," she shouted angrily. "I didn't. I didn't get out of bed last night, it would have been too cold, and I wouldn't have been able to find my slippers in the dark anyway. And I wasn't playing that stupid old piano. It must have been the ghost."

And that's when they both stopped talking at the same time and just looked at each other, stunned by what they were both thinking.

Grandma spoke first. "I'm sorry. It's not a stupid old piano. It's a beautiful piano. It's the most beautiful piano I've ever seen. And if I were a ghost, I'd want to come back and play it too."

Charlotte-the-housemaid looked stricken. She walked around the corner, Grandma following, just to look at the piano. It stood alone at the other end of the room. The morning sun gave it a silvery-gray sheen.

"I dunno. Doesn't look all that ghostly to me," said Charlotte-the-housemaid, but not very convincingly.

"Maybe it's only ghostly at night," said Grandma. Then she added, "In the daylight, it just looks magical. Maybe it's not haunted, maybe it's enchanted. Maybe that's why the ghost comes back? Because it reminds her of what made her happy in life...?"

"Well," said Charlotte-the-housemaid, "The Missus did like to laugh a lot. You can see it in her eyes. In both paintings."

"So there," said Grandma, as if that proved something. "I'm not going to be afraid of any ghost who plays the piano and neither should you."

"It's still a ghost," said Charlotte-the-housemaid.

"We're all ghosts," Grandma decided. "We just ride around in meat and skeletons until we're tired of them. Then, we leave them behind and go on without."

"Is that what you say?" asked Charlotte-the-housemaid.

"Yes, that's what I say, because that's what I think." Grandma folded her arms and put on her stubborn face.

"Well, all right then." Charlotte-the-housemaid was smart enough not to argue with Grandma. Instead, she said, "But in the meantime, let's ask the ghost to please not play too loud in the night, so she won't wake up Cook and have her blame you. All right?"

"All right," said Grandma. "I will. In fact, I'll even write her a note. Will that do?"

"If it works for The Missus, it works for me. Good on ya, then."

Grandma wrote a very nice letter, thanking The Missus for letting her play the piano, but very politely asking her not to play loud enough to wake anyone up. She signed it and put it on the music rack so the ghost wouldn't miss it. Then, satisfied that she had behaved properly, she began looking through all the scores on the shelves.

For most of the afternoon, Grandma sat on the floor sorting through stacks of sheet music. There were popular songs and ballads, concertos and suites, even Franz Liszt's transcriptions of Beethoven's nine symphonies. There were piano concertos by Mozart, Grieg, Tchaikovsky, and of course Beethoven again. And surprise, there were even some Scott Joplin ragtime numbers. Most of the classical pieces had too many pages and looked very complicated and difficult, but Grandma was excited to see such complex melodies and harmonies captured on paper. She wanted to hear how they sounded, but she couldn't pick which one to try first. Whatever she chose, she knew it would be a lot of work – and take a lot of practice.

Finally, she settled on Beethoven's "Pathetique" sonata, not the whole piece, but the second movement, because it was slow and wistful. Grandma said she liked wistful music, and that's why "The Aquarium" was her favorite, but I think she just liked slow music because it was easier to play than fast music.

Grandma explained to us that when she was just beginning, she invented her own way of practicing. She'd take two or three bars of music and play them over and over and over, like she was teaching her fingers to find out where all the notes were on the keyboard. Then she'd go on to the next two or three bars and play them over and over the same way. When she reached the end of the page, she'd go back to the beginning and play the whole page over and over until she felt she could get through it comfortably. Grandma said she had to learn a piece of music one note at a time, one bar at a time, one page at a time. It must have worked because I never heard her miss a note.

Once I asked her how she played the piano so well. She just smiled and said, "All you have to do is hit the keys in the right order. The piano does the rest." But I don't think Grandma ever noticed how hard she worked at the keyboard because she was always too busy concentrating. When she played the piano, she puckered up her face in a terrible frown, focusing as hard as she could to touch every key just right.

That day, she practiced the "Pathetique" all day long, just the second movement. Played at the right tempo, it should only be five minutes long, but Grandma was still finding her way through it and playing it very slowly. She didn't notice how much time had passed until the room had turned rosy with sunset and Charlotte-the-housemaid came in to call her to dinner. Beans and potatoes and bits of ham and cheese on toast.

That was when Grandma realized they had skipped tea. That only happened when something bad occurred and everybody was so upset they just stopped in shock.

There was terrible news of the war. There was news every night, and sometimes music too, sad or triumphant – or music that was supposed to be inspiring. But this evening, the news was very bad. The radio in the kitchen spoke in many serious voices. Grandma forgot all about Ludwig van Beethoven and his marvelous concerto.

The night before, German planes had bombed the town of Coventry. The voices on the radio said that thousands of buildings had been destroyed. Hundreds of people had been killed, including many women and children. It could have been much worse, but most of the town's residents had escaped death and injury in Coventry's air-raid shelters.

Cook was grim-faced and red-eyed as if she had been crying all day. Charlotte-the-housemaid stomped around like an angry bull. The groundskeeper came slamming in, stared around the room for a moment, saw three children sitting wide-eyed and afraid at the kitchen table, then slammed out again without saying a word, probably because the words he wanted to say weren't fit for children's ears.

Coventry was only 160 miles south of Durham. Grandma said she didn't have a good sense of distance at that age, but she got the feeling that Coventry was close enough that the people in Durham were worried they might be targeted tonight. Cook and Charlotte-the-housemaid talked back and forth that maybe everyone should move down to the basement for shelter and sleep there a few nights, but Charlotte-the-housemaid said that there were several good air raid sirens in the town, loud enough to wake everyone up. If there was an air raid, they'd all hear them in plenty of time to go down to the root cellar or the basement, so everybody should sleep in their own beds tonight and not be afraid of some silly Nazi bogeyman.

It turned into a terrible argument between Cook and Charlotte-the-housemaid, without either of them ever saying the words specifically – "the safety of the children" – but finally Charlotte-the-housemaid won out. She said she had already made up enough beds today, she wasn't going to make up any more in the basement. Cook said she'd go down and sleep in the basement anyway. Charlotte-the-housemaid said Cook could go sleep in Carfax Abbey for all she cared. That made Cook very angry and she stormed out of the kitchen. Grandma and her younger siblings laughed at that, even though they didn't know why Carfax Abbey was so funny, but for many days afterward, "go to Carfax Abbey" was their way of saying "go to the bad place."

Grandma didn't go back to the piano after dinner. Charlotte-the-housemaid read them a story from Beatrix Potter – about a rabbit named Peter who got himself into some terrible trouble in Mr. McGregor's garden, but still got out all right and came home to a nice cup of chamomile tea. Not Grandma's favorite story, she would have preferred *The Wind in the Willows*, but her younger brother and sister liked it, so she sat with them and listened quietly.

After the story, Charlotte-the-housemaid decided to take the two younger children down to the basement for the night after all. Despite her earlier objections, she had made up three beds, but Grandma said she wanted to stay upstairs with the piano. Charlotte-the-housemaid said she might allow this only if Grandma promised to come down to the basement immediately if the air raid sirens sounded. Grandma agreed.

There was no air raid that night, but Grandma woke up anyway. She thought she heard something – music. Someone was playing the piano, very softly.

It was the "Pathetique" sonata. Second movement. Not too fast, not too slow. Not the way Grandma had practiced it, but the way it should be played – the way a master pianist would play it, turning the dispassionate notes on the page into breathtaking moments of emotion. Grandma sat up in bed and listened, enchanted – and too appreciative to get out of bed to see who was at the keyboard. And yes, maybe she was a little bit scared as well. After all, no one else in the house could play the piano – certainly not like this. It had to be the ghost.

Grandma listened while the ghost – or whoever it was – played the whole sonata, not just the second movement. Some people, Grandma said, play the sonata ferociously, like they're angry. Grandma admitted she plays it that way when she's angry, but the "Pathetique" sonata isn't about anger. It's about grief. It's about loss. It's about the terrible feeling of emptiness that scourges your soul when you've lost that very special someone you love so much it hurts all the way down to the bottom. It's about the rage you feel inside because there's nothing you can do to recover yourself – and it's about accepting that the past is gone forever. It's about coming to terms with whatever is still left to you, however meager it is.

And – Grandma said, this was her interpretation – it's also about saying goodbye, because life is one long process of saying goodbye, over and over and over, until it's your turn to go. When she said that, I realized for the first time just how much she must still miss Grandpa. Even after all these years.

Grandma said she didn't know if there were ghosts or not, but maybe sometimes some part of a person's spirit is so strong that it can't die. It stays in the world for a long while, only fading away slowly as time and memory evaporate. Maybe that's why she heard music in the night – it was the part of the lady that couldn't die, couldn't go away yet.

In the morning, there was more news about Coventry, about rescue workers going in, about recovering the bodies, many of them so badly burned that identification was impossible. Four hundred dead, maybe more, they wouldn't know for sure for days, not until they finished digging through the wreckage. Hundreds more injured. The whole town reduced to rubble. A terrible disaster. Another reason to hate the monsters on the other side of the Channel. The monsters were already bragging about how effective their war machines had been against Coventry and how even more destructive they would be when they turned their attention back to London.

Cook burned the eggs and toast. Charlotte-the-housemaid was unusually quiet. She hushed the children sternly when they started to giggle about something. Everyone was upset about everything. The groundskeeper was nowhere to be found – he'd probably gone into town and gotten raging drunk like a lot of the other old men, especially those who'd survived the Great War, he was probably still sleeping it off somewhere. Fortunately, the November weather was still unseasonably mild – mild enough that if he'd fallen asleep in an alley or passed out behind the pub, at least he wouldn't have frozen to death.

Later, when Charlotte-the-housemaid was making up the beds, Grandma asked her if she had heard any of the music in the night. Charlotte-the-housemaid shook her head. "Too much hurt and too much sorrow, sweetheart. I took a pill to help me sleep. You could have played the *1812 Overture* with real cannons and it wouldn't have roused me."

That afternoon, Charlotte-the-housemaid, Cook, and the groundskeeper all went into town, carrying bundles of clothes, sheets for bandages, blankets, and anything else they could find to help the survivors of Coventry. They took the two younger children with them, but Grandma said she wasn't feeling well and Charlotte-the-housemaid thought she did look poorly, so after another argument between Cook and Charlotte-the-housemaid, Grandma was allowed to stay behind.

As soon as they left, she went straight to her room and the shelves behind the piano. She sat down on the floor and began sorting through the sheet music. She did want to go back to the "Pathetique" and begin learning the other two movements, especially now that she had heard the sonata the way it should be played. But at the same time, she wanted to try something different, something that wasn't so sad. She didn't have the right word for it, she said – not then – but she wanted to play something that wouldn't hurt to hear, something that would make the tears all right. Something peaceful, something that would be an island of calm in her small, troubled world.

She finally settled on another Beethoven sonata, Piano Sonata No. 14 in C-sharp minor, the "Moonlight" sonata. The first movement. It's slow and it has its own wistful quality, but the way Grandma plays the piece, it's about the shimmering reflection of the moon on the surface of a quiet lake, somewhere high in the mountains. Maybe there are snowcapped peaks visible, both in the distance and seen upside down in the silent water. The music is about a woman, or maybe a man, sitting on the shore, staring out over the barely rippling waters, reflecting on her own life, her past, her future, her possibilities. She's at peace with her choices. It's a moment of contemplation, maybe even contentment, before she goes back to the brighter world that waits when dawn comes again.

Cook had left a cold plate for Grandma in the kitchen, in case everyone had to stay in town to help with the rescue efforts for Coventry. They wouldn't know how much needed to be done until the emergency teams reported back – so if there were sheets to be torn for bandages or boxes of food to be packed, they might need to spend the night helping. Grandma had decided the ghost wasn't going to hurt anyone, so she wasn't afraid to spend the night by herself, but she had to spend a lot of time reassuring Charlotte-the-housemaid that she would be all right and that she could take care of herself.

After she ate, she returned to the piano. She had set aside a whole stack of music that interested her. "Au Claire de Lune," of course, and Erik Satie's *Gymnopedie No. 1*, and "Solace" by Scott Joplin. She'd heard of Mr. Joplin, she'd even heard some of his music in films, but she'd been told by her piano teacher that Mr. Joplin's music was not for polite society, and certainly not for little girls. Her teacher had not explained why. So when Grandma found the music for "Solace," she definitely had to put it in the growing stack of pieces she wanted to learn.

She also found Bach's Prelude and Fugue in C major, which was also the accompaniment to Gounaud's Ave Maria, and maybe that would be a good thing to practice too, considering what had happened in Coventry. She added Mozart's Piano Sonata No. 16 in C major, the first movement, Bach's Minuet in G major from the *Notebook for Anna Magdalena Bach*, and was looking at Chopin's Polonaise in A Major, trying to decide if it might be too difficult, when she noticed the piece immediately below it – George Gershwin's *Rhapsody in Blue*.

She knew it would be much too difficult for her, but she couldn't resist. Maybe there was a piece of it, even a little bit, that she could learn. She took it to the piano, sat down with it, and turned the pages back and forth, frowning. She'd never seen music like this before. She tried a few phrases. Her hands weren't big enough for some of the chords, but she really wanted to know what the music would sound like. She'd heard it on the radio once, before the war, when they'd still lived in London, and she'd sat before the speaker, mesmerized by the dramatic syncopation. *Rhapsody in Blue* was one of the reasons she'd wanted to learn how to play the piano. And now, here in her hands, she finally had the music. How could she not want to play it?

Grandma said it wasn't the hardest piece of music she ever had to learn, but it was the hardest piece of music she ever tried to play – because she wanted so much to get it right. There were parts of it that she just couldn't manage, not yet, but there were a few places where she did evoke a small sense of Gershwin's magic.

At last, though, she had to put it aside. She turned her attention instead to "Solace" by Mr. Scott Joplin. Although it was ragtime, it was a more thoughtful exploration of the form than anything she had heard before. Grandma worked her way through it carefully, paying special attention to the recurring phrase that suggested a quiet stroll in a garden, or perhaps a pleasant carriage ride through a shady green.

When the great clock in the hall struck eleven, Grandma realized she had stayed up much later than she was supposed to. Reluctantly, she closed the fallboard and went to bed, wondering if the ghost would show up and play this very modern music.

The way Grandma tells it, she was so tired, she slept through the entire night. But she had a dream, and in her dream there was music – marvelous music. She was standing alone in a great room, a golden hall, and in the distance, there was the piano all gleaming and white, just as it had been when it was new, and sitting at the keyboard, a beautiful woman in a beautiful white gown, so elegant and gracious, her hands dancing across the keys almost too fast to see. And the music she was playing – it was the most exquisite music Grandma had ever heard.

And then the woman finished the piece. She stopped, she rested her hands lightly on her lap for a moment, then she closed the fallboard to indicate she was done. She looked up from the piano, she looked directly down the length of the room to Grandma...and smiled and nodded. Then she stood up, she wasn't tall, but she wasn't short. She wasn't thin and she wasn't fat – she had the stoutness of age and the grace of confidence. Her white hair was piled high in a bun and that made her look taller than five feet. Then she turned and left the room, disappearing into the shuttered French doors as if they weren't there, passing through them to a place that wasn't on the other side.

In the morning, Grandma fixed herself tea and toast with jam for breakfast. Cook and Charlotte-the-housemaid and the groundskeeper showed up shortly before noon, tired but satisfied they had made a difference. Grandma's younger brother and sister were excited to tell her about everything they had seen in Durham proper. All the inns and hotels were full to overcrowded, so they had stayed overnight with Cook's daughter, everyone sleeping on the floor in front of a huge open fireplace.

Many people in Durham had opened their homes to the refugees from Coventry, and there were lorries and buses going back and forth all day and night. People arrived on every train, still black from the smoke of the fires, many of them carrying what little they could salvage from their burned-out homes. Some people had to be carried from the train on stretchers. The hospitals were already full, but more and more injured were arriving with every train. There were so many people arriving in Durham, they were sleeping on the floor of the college gymnasium.

Later, when Charlotte-the-housemaid got around to asking Grandma if she had managed all right, Grandma said she had. When Charlotte-the-housemaid came into her room to make up her bed, Grandma asked her about the sheet music on the shelves. Did she know where it had all come from?

"Oh my, yes," said Charlotte-the-housemaid. "Before the war, Mister and Missus went to London regularly, sometimes twice a month. Every time there was an important concert or show, they took the train down. Sometimes, the Mister was already in London and Missus had to travel alone, so I went along with her when she needed a travel maid. I went with Missus to her favorite music stores. Oh, such a lady she was. She picked through the music as if she could hear it with her eyes. Sometimes, she would sit at the piano in the store and play a piece to see how it sounded. Everyone in the store would stop and listen. Oh my, you should have seen how the clerks loved her. Everyone did. Wherever she went, it was a concert. And then we'd come back home with her luggage full of music – every trip, and sometimes mine too if there wasn't enough room in hers – oh, we had such fun. Missus was a very famous pianist, she played all over Europe, even for some of the crowned heads, she did. Missus had trained with some of the very best teachers in Vienna and Berlin, but she had a – oh, what would you call it? She had a wonderful curiosity, a fascination with all the new music coming from America. She said it was very exciting what the American composers were creating, that they were inventing new kinds of music. I'm sure she could hear things I couldn't, it all sounded like music to me, but when she sat down to play, you just wanted to stop and listen. Oh, listen to me now, I'm starting to sound like I know what I'm talking about. I'm getting above myself, but...well, I did love traveling with her. Whenever I went with, we would sit together and she would very patiently explain the music to me, what it was about, and why it was important. It wasn't just that it made the train rides feel like no time at all was passing – it was like we were just two old friends chatting away. She was a dear woman, she treated everyone the same, it didn't matter if you were a lady or a servant. Oh, and she had the most delicious way of speaking – such a thick accent, all German and Jewish, what they call Yiddish, it was great fun to listen to her talk – and she always looked so elegant, until she opened her mouth and sounded like a – like a Russian babushka. The Mister worshipped her so much. He had the same accent, only thicker than hers, so to listen to them chatter back and forth – especially if they were disagreeing about the details of some silly little thing that had happened in Düsseldorf or was it Straussburg or maybe it was Brussels, no I'm sure it was Marseilles, because there was that little café that served those funny little cakes you liked so much, until finally he would look across at her and say with such a twinkle, yes whatever, my dear, I'm sure you are right, his way of saying he loved her too much to argue. They were so cute, they were. Oh my, we all miss them every day. This big old house is too empty without them." Then Charlotte-the-housemaid patted Grandma on the head. "It's been so much better since you arrived. All of us like having someone to take care of."

Then Grandma remembered something from her dream. She pointed to the shuttered French doors at the west side of the room, behind the piano. "What's out there?" she asked.

"Oh, that was Missus' own private garden...." Charlotte-the-housemaid said. "She would go out there with the Mister whenever he came back from London. The two of them would just sit with each other, holding hands like a couple of newlyweds, and catch up on all the things they wanted to share. They were such a perfect pair, him with his cane and all, and she – oh my, she always dressed herself up for him like it was the most special day of their lives, she always dressed in white – you can see that in her pictures – she always said a lady should be a lady, if you know what I mean, except at the piano, she said, where a pianist should be everything from a delightful sparkle to a ferocious monsoon. I think that's why she liked playing the piano so much – because it let her be everything she couldn't be inside a corset and a white dress. She liked to bust loose, she did."

"Can we open those big French doors?" Grandma asked.

Charlotte-the-housemaid hesitated. "Those doors haven't been opened since –" She took another breath. "Missus is buried out there. In her garden. The Mister won't go out there anymore. I think maybe he wants to believe she's still here in the house."

"I think we should open the doors and let the sunlight in. It's too dark and gloomy in here."

"Yes, it is, but –"

"But the Mister isn't here, is he? And maybe the ghost doesn't want to feel locked out? Maybe ghosts are ghosts because they're lonely? Maybe she misses him as much as he misses her?"

Grandma pushed past Charlotte-the-housemaid and began unlatching the big French doors. Charlotte-the-housemaid fussed a little more, but made no move to stop Grandma from throwing open the doors to let in the sunset. Wide steps led down to a circle of precisely trimmed rose bushes, where a few red and pink and white flowers still bloomed, even this late in the year.

Charlotte-the-housemaid followed Grandma down the steps, past the bushes, past a circle of benches around a pond and a fountain, to a quiet hedged-in sanctuary and a simple marble monolith. Carved into the face of it was the outline of a grand piano, and below that, a name and two dates.

"This is where she rests," Charlotte-the-housemaid whispered.

"Only in the daytime," Grandma said with the certainty only a young lady could have. "At night she likes to play the piano."

Charlotte-the-housemaid looked at Grandma with a raised eyebrow. Was Grandma making something up or did she believe what she just said?

Grandma turned to the marker and said, "Please come back and play some more. I want to learn to play as well as you." Then she turned back to Charlotte-the-housemaid. "This is a very pretty garden. I think I would like to come out here just to sit and enjoy the day, wouldn't you? I don't think the Missus would mind if we came back. Everything you tell me about her, she must have been very nice." Then Grandma remembered her manners and said, "Maybe sometime, we could have tea out here? For the Missus?"

That night, after dinner, after the radio concert, after she was washed and brushed and ready for bed, Grandma went to the piano part of the room and picked up all the music she had set aside for herself. She put the pages on top of the piano, spreading them out in a fan so all the titles were visible.

Then she sat down on the bench and waited. She must have dozed for a while. But then suddenly, she was awake. And there, sitting next to her, was a kindly-looking, white-haired old lady – a little bit transparent, but very real.

Grandma didn't know what to say, but the ghost did.

"So, dah-link. Vat vould you like to play tonight?"

Grandma said it so perfectly, we laughed and laughed and snuggled in next to her, still giggling. After that, all Grandma had to say was, "So, dah-link. Vat vould you like to play?" and we would all start laughing again.

But finally, I asked, "Was that a made-up story? Just to make us feel better?"

Grandma gave me the Grandma look, offended. "I never make up anything. Every word of it was true."

The next morning, we dressed up in our best clothes and went to Mama's funeral. It was very somber. And very sad. But neither I nor Emma cried. Everybody said we were very brave, but we knew better. There was nothing to be sad about. Mama was still with us. Laughing quietly in a way that only we could hear.

I still have my mother's old blue nightgown in my drawer, just a keepsake now. Sometimes, when I'm feeling lonely, sometimes when I'm feeling down, I take it out and hold it against my cheek. It reminds me of a time when I felt safe. It reminds me of people long gone, even a lady I never met.

Tonight, I didn't close the bedroom door. Tonight, I left it open.

And tonight, I did not hear something scratching. Instead, I heard music.

I don't have a piano, I gave up playing years ago.

But Grandma never stopped.

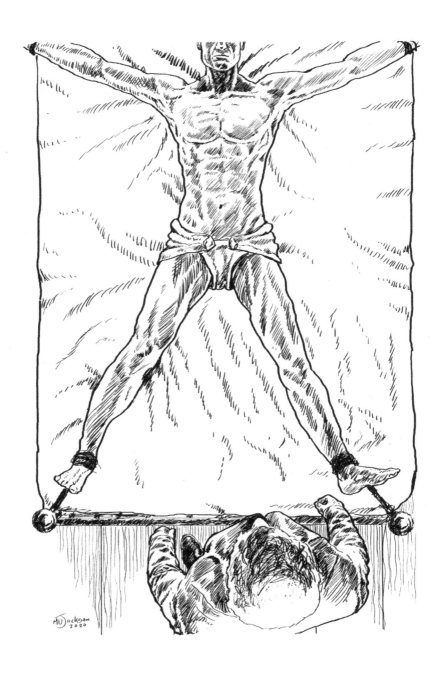

Jacob in Manhattan

Lying naked on the bed, next to Jacob's porcelain body, the blankets tangled at our feet, I listen to the sound of my own breathing. Sweat tingles on my skin. My heart still pounds.

"That's it?"

"That's it," he confirms.

"I thought I was supposed to drink your blood."

"Body fluids. It's all the same. This was a lot more fun, wasn't it?"

I have to smile. I can still taste him.

Morning growls at the window, the curtains drawn to keep it at bay. There's a stain on the ceiling shaped like a dog's head. I feel a strange hollowness within myself. I touch my heart.

"Is this it? Has it started?"

"No. Not yet." Jacob rolls onto his side, facing me. He puts a cold hand over mine, listening to the frantic beat inside. "You're scared –?"

"Yes, I am. I don't know what I've done, and it's too late to change my mind, isn't it?"

"Way too late. You're committed." Jacob laughs gently. "It's like the first time you get into bed, naked, with another man. It's scary and delicious, both at once. This is the same thing, only more so." He leans toward me, I turn halfway to meet his embrace and he kisses me. He pulls me close, wrapping me in his arms. "It'll be all right. I promise."

He holds me for a long time, long enough for me to feel his heart beating against mine. We synchronize emotionally and physically, a strange sensation. Finally, when we are both complete in the moment and ready for the next, he releases me back to the rumpled sheets. The dog's head stain has an open mouth. He's panting too...? Or is he smiling, laughing? He saw the whole thing, the frantic scrambling of two naked bodies rocking together, the coupling and uncoupling and recoupling. What does the dog head think?

Do I care? It's just a stain on the ceiling. Water? How did it get there? It looks old. Is it a reminder of some long-passed storm that ripped away part of the roof and pissed its wrath into the structure below? Do I care? No.

I glance back to Jacob. He studies me with shining eyes.

"So...when will it happen?"

"It's already happening. You're just not going to feel it for a while."

"How long?"

"Hard to say. Depends on your metabolism." He smiles and his eyes gleam with a strange kind of inner light. Desire? Insight? Knowledge? Amusement? How does he do that? I can't look away. The silence grows with a dark intensity, a sense of something impending.

I have to speak – not to speak, but to break the moment. It's too intense. Whatever is rushing down on us, I need to postpone it a moment longer. "Um –"

"What?"

"Um – nothing." Anything. "You were right. The sex was fantastic."

He laughs softly, a quiet sound, barely audible. He traces his fingers down the center of my chest, down through the few brave strands of masculine identity – as if he's tasting them with his touch.

"That's just the beginning. It gets better."

"I can't imagine it."

"That's right. You can't. Not yet."

I listen to the sound of my breathing. I listen to his inhalations and exhalations as well, trying to decipher meaning. What is he thinking right now?

I'm impatient. I want to see the rest of the spectrum. I want to hear the higher sounds, the lower ones. I want to smell the things I'm missing and feel all the sensations I've never known. Everything he promised.

Jacob still studies me, reading me, watching the way my feelings flicker across my face, revealing all the internal processes, both physical and emotional. He seems fascinated.

"What are you doing?"

"Watching you change."

"I thought you said –"

"Not the physical. The emotional. There are steps – all the way from fear to anger to curiosity, eventually acceptance and ownership. You're still at fear."

I look inside. It's a trick I learned at the keyboard – all that writing, all that typing. The only soul you have to examine is your own. Jacob is right. I am afraid.

"I never asked – will it hurt?"

"Does being born hurt? Does sex hurt? It all hurts – it upsets your equilibrium. But if you choose to enjoy the hurt, then it doesn't hurt at all. It's…it's something else. Something beyond pleasure."

"Okay."

"Here…" He lets his hand – his pale porcelain fingers – explore my chest, my belly, then back up again to gently tweak a nipple. "First you're going to feel cold. Very cold. So cold you'll l think you're dying. And that's when the fear will kick in. The panic. The first terrifying reactions of horror – it's really happening. The adrenaline will flow and you'll start sweating. Cold first, then hot. Hotter. Very hot. Hotter than that. Feverish. You'll feel like you're on fire. You'll smell your flesh burning, you'll hear the crackling sounds of transformation inside, you'll see red and orange flames scouring your body, inside and out – because all your nerve endings will be tingling at once.

"You'll get into a cold tub and it won't be cold enough. You'll see steam rising off your skin. Real? Or another hallucination? You won't know. That's why I'm here. To ease you through it. You'll hold onto me, screaming, crying, raging. You'll probably try to beat me – you'll be furious that I've put you through this. You'll be delirious. You'll see me as a monster – and then you'll see me as your lover again – and then you'll want to abandon yourself to delicious sex with the monster. Your body will be racked with ferocious energies –

"Yes, Joseph – it'll hurt, it'll be the worst hurt you ever felt – but it'll be a good hurt – like stretching, like waking up, but it'll still hurt. And you'll cry. You'll weep, you'll sob, you'll howl in anguish. And because all your nerve cells are firing, you're going to hallucinate – like the worst and greatest drug trip ever. Dazzling fluorescent colors, all shifting and twisting. Amazing sounds, a symphony of contradictions. And the smells, the cacophony of odors. All of that. And the physical feelings, too. Everything. You'll feel your skin from the inside – you'll taste the way your organs slide against each other, how they work, the ferocious balance of this against that – all the flavors of hormones and enzymes, sugars and amino acids and everything else. Oh – and you'll feel dizzy, like you're flying, falling, turning every which way, tumbling into a bottomless well of fear and despair, curiosity and wonder, amazement and regret –"

"Until –?"

"Until you're exhausted. Until you have expended every last particle of energy you have to draw upon. You'll collapse. Your heart will slow. Slower than normal. And your breathing will get shallower, very shallow. You'll get cold. Cold as death. You might panic, thinking you're going to die. But there won't be any energy left. You'll be so empty you won't even have the strength to die. So you'll just go...call it dormant. But it's not that either. You'll be conscious, just conscious enough to know that you're not dead yet – not yet. You'll be hovering just above death –"

"But I'm not going to die...?"

"No. Not while I'm here."

"Some people do?"

"Yes. Some bodies don't have the strength to survive the transition. You do. You will. Now listen to me – when it starts, when you're going through all these feelings, it's going to be scary, delicious, confusing all at once. Just keep remembering, keep saying, 'This is what Jacob told me would happen. This is part of it.' Keep reminding yourself of that. It's all part of the process. You don't have to scared. Just experience it. Enjoy it. Be it. Own it. I know these words don't make sense – try it this way. Whatever you're feeling, look into the heart of the feeling, look as deep into it as you can, dive into it, be the feeling. The whole feeling, ferociously, passionately, completely. Okay? And whenever you need to reach out for me, I'll be there holding your hand, talking you through it. Can you do that –?"

His eyes are intense. I nod. "I'll do it for you, yes."

"No!" He's suddenly angry. "Do it for yourself. Be everything you can see and hear and touch and feel – everything. That way, when you come out on the far side, all of that will belong to you."

He squeezes my hand too hard, his strength is incredible. "You're hurting me –"

"Yes, I am –" How much fury burns behind his eyes!

"Jacob, you're starting to scare me –"

"Good." For a moment, the pain is impossible – and then the intensity finally breaks. He lets go and pulls back. "You need to know this, Joseph. I'm not doing this to you. You chose this. You are doing this yourself. You're going to be all alone in there. You can die – or you can come back. It's up to you."

"So, you're saying I could die...?"

"You could. If you choose it. If you give up. If you let the panic overwhelm you. If you choose to control it, if you remember that you're the owner of everything that happens to you – you'll endure it long enough for your body to start rebuilding itself. You'll be dormant for a long time, but I'll be here watching you, keeping you safe. And if you can remember that –" He takes my hand again, this time not so hard.

Something clicks.

"You've done this before, haven't you?"

Jacob doesn't answer. Not right away. But his expression shifts, darkens – I've caused him to remember.

"Yes," he finally admits. "You're not the first."

"So there were others before me?"

"Yes, there were."

"Where are they? What happened to them?"

"They died."

"They died –?"

"Yes. We can die. Sometimes we get caught, not very often though. Usually, if a Nightsider dies…it's because another Nightsider killed him."

"And yours? The ones you created –?"

"Ahh. That's a different story –"

"Tell me?"

"You really want to hear this?"

"Yes, I do."

"You won't like it."

"All the more reason to tell me."

Jacob laughs. "You might be right." He rolls over onto his back, stares at the ceiling. "Okay –"

I was living in New York. This was long after Monsieur had died. I had an apartment in the village. Greenwich Village. It was just outside the boundaries of polite society. Bohemians and artists and sexual perverts lived in the village. So it was the perfect cover.

I was almost 90 years old, 88. I looked maybe 25 – in the dark anyway. In the light, you might have seen the faint patina of lines at the edges of my eyes, but few people ever saw me in bright light, and never daylight. So I passed for young. I still do.

I had considerable resources, not just the initial inheritance I had received from Monsieur, but quite a bit of my own as well. It turned out that the original amount I had received when I first was led to believe that Monsieur had perished in a fire was only a small fraction of his holdings. It was the amount that he had given lawyer Durant to manage. But there were other lawyers, other holdings, other identities. A dozen, maybe two. Monsieur was over two hundred years old. You don't get that old by accident. You learn a lot of ways to protect yourself.

Nightsiders cannot maintain any identity much longer than a decade. People start to wonder why you're not aging. After the umpteenth joke about a painting in the attic, it's time to move on. So a Nightsider maintains multiple identities and multiple properties in as many cities as he can afford. Most of the time, he's an absentee landlord, but every few years, he sends his "son" to live in a new city, and the lawyers who manage those holdings are instructed to manage his accounts. From time to time, the absentee landlord passes away and the "son" inherits the properties, and rearranges the management to suit himself until it's time for the next progression and the Nightsider moves on to a third city, and a fourth.

To any investigating agency, I was merely a renter in one of the more elegant and respected buildings in the neighborhood. The building was owned by a small property-management firm, which also managed properties in the Bronx, Queens, Harlem, Brooklyn and several spacious brownstones on the upper east side, just off Park Avenue.

Every quarter, the company sent a profit-and-loss statement, plus a sizable check to a downtown corporation, which distributed the earnings to its various shareholders. Several of those shareholders were companies based in other states. They distributed their earnings monthly, quarterly, or annually to other companies and other shareholders. Eventually, after passing through at least a dozen shell companies, some of the funds would arrive at my current lawyer's office, and the rest to the offices of other lawyers in other cities. Most of the time, the lawyers and the executives managing the various properties were scrupulously honest. Several times they were not.

I wish I could report that lawyers are an acquired taste. They are not. They taste of dust and dogma. They are oatmeal.

But that's a different discussion, which we will have another time. I was speaking of my apartment in the village. It was small and comfortable, a retreat from the responsibilities of a larger domain. Many of the furnishings were leftovers from an earlier time, dating as far back as the turn of the century. The twentieth was a century of escalating horrors, a delicious era. The first half, anyway.

The war in Europe had ended, but the war in the Pacific was dragging on. War-weary combat troops were arriving from England and France and Italy by the shipload, almost every day – and just as fast, they were loaded onto westbound trains, where they would be loaded onto other ships – headed for some unknown island base from which the invasion of Japan would ultimately be launched. Everyone expected it to be a hard, brutal campaign. Perhaps a million casualties. No one knew.

So, even this far away – even at this remove, the city was a pressure cooker of uncertainty, a mixture of giddiness and fear. There were good times ahead – but maybe there weren't. The Japanese weren't like the Germans. The Germans had momentarily succumbed to the insane fantasies of a madman, but the Japanese had invested centuries in the conviction that their emperor was the living son of heaven. The Imperial Sovereign was much more than a political delusion. He was the nation. Americans were having trouble understanding this – it was too alien.

So down in the streets, the mood was alternately grave and manic, depending on the hour.

Daytime, people went about their business, rushing to work, rushing home, rushing to the store, rushing to spend their ration coupons on butter and eggs.

Nighttime, however, as the storefronts shuttered, as the office buildings locked up, a different world began. The later it got, the more interesting the night became. Darker buildings beckoned. Shadowy doorways flickered open, briefly revealing red-lit spaces within. Silhouettes moved together. It was heaven.

This particular June night, I wasn't hungry, I wasn't anything – I was restless. The night was hot and humid, the city stank of sweat and garbage – there was no magic anywhere. But it wasn't the city, it was me. I recognized the feeling, it was a different kind of hunger. When you're that old, even novelty isn't novelty anymore, it's just a different way of recycling the past. When you're that old, you don't look for newness, you look for nuance.

Eventually, I gravitated to a midtown bar – not one I'd visited often, I didn't like the flavors of humanity here. They swirled around me as if I didn't exist. I understood why. Mostly servicemen – they were still unfolding themselves from the rigors of the war. They didn't know how to talk to anyone who hadn't been over there. So I chatted with the bartender.

He had a friendly smile, not just a professional one – he actually enjoyed his work. He flashed a flirtatious grin and slid a beer in front of me without my even asking.

Maybe his name was Bud. Everybody called him that, but I got the feeling it was only a nickname. He wore a black silk shirt and a red bow tie – and a gold ring in his right earlobe. Did he know the meaning of that? I'd grown up in Seattle in the 1860s. A fisherman wore a gold earring in case he died – the earring would pay the undertaker for his burial.

I doubted that Bud knew that particular history. Apparently, in this world – this place where men sought intimacy with other men – apparently, it meant something else, I wasn't sure. I hadn't kept up with the nuances of this subculture, but I was charmed by it. Bud was proud of his difference. That should have been a warning, but I wasn't paying attention to my own senses. Or maybe I was enchanted by his silk shirt – it suggested he had a sensual side.

I admit, I was preoccupied, not just that evening, but for several weeks preceding. Although the tumultuous circumstances of my own recent past had been resolved, albeit not as smoothly as I had intended, my designs for the future remained uncharted. I was unfocused and still circling through my thoughts, rehearsing all the mistakes I'd made, as well as my fumbled recovery, wondering how I had stumbled into that situation and if there had been any possibility of extricating myself more effectively than the clumsy way I had finally resorted to. Only the urgencies of the moment, the influx and transshipment of massive numbers of troops and all the mishaps and miseries that inevitably accompanied such a circumstance, had spared me a closer examination by the local authorities.

This internal conversation had been continuing long enough to become an annoying loop, a broken record of repetition. Night after night, I had fled from the cage of my apartment seeking redemption, and if not that, anything else that would distract me from another evening of relentless self-absorption.

As chance would have it –

Bud's casual flirtations were essentially meaningless, but for the moment I played the innocent again. I was doing post-graduate work at NYU, or I was here on business from St. Loo, or maybe I was just another lonely soul, out on his own for the night and looking for an illicit thrill – a dalliance, a bit of sexual adventure to prove that I was still young and virile and attractive. Or perhaps I was once again just another college boy from Boston, all alone in the big city.

Whatever. I let Bud flirt with me and I smiled in appreciation. I was flattered at the attention. Men of our nature do not flirt in the same manner that men of another nature flirt with women. It is a dance of meanings, both deliberate and casual, it is a testing of intention – playful banter disguising a very real negotiation. It is the construction of a different kind of relationship than exists in the more common world.

In the larger domain of humanity, when two men meet, there's a brief flicker of hesitation. They size each other up. The unspoken question is "Can I take him?" Sometimes they test each other – the relationship remains unresolved for as long as it takes to determine which of the two will be the stronger, which will lead and which will follow. If the question never gets resolved, the men become rivals, enemies in a constant state of opposition.

But when men of a different nature meet, the unspoken question is not one of opposition, but intimacy. "Can I take him?" exists in a vastly different context. It becomes, "Do I want to be naked with him?" Not just physically naked, but emotionally as well.

And yes, it is that same emotional nakedness that Nightsiders still crave – even after a century or more of life. Everything else is just cardboard dancers moving against a flattened panorama – as unconvincing as a theatrical backdrop. It does not have to include a sexual intimacy, but when it's possible –

And in that moment, I allowed myself to be charmed by Bud's easy flirtations. When he said, "Stick around. I get off at midnight," I was charmed. I said, "I'd like that."

No, I was not hungry – not for that. That's another assumption that daysiders make – that Nightsiders are only interested in feeding. We are not. Well, at least, I am not. I am not a glutton. There are too many other pleasures in life, and with the enhanced senses of my condition, even the simplest of flavors can be a joyous delight. Vanilla ice cream? Most people just eat it – never truly tasting the complex ballet of flavor and texture and temperature. If you take the time to savor its delicacy, it can be as filled with discovery as a seven-course banquet.

The same is true of the other senses, particularly that frenzied grappling for position that passes for sexual connection. The way that sexual relations are portrayed in cinema – it's a pernicious lie, a fable for the impoverished souls who hunger for intimacy and accept physicality as a poor substitute. What is portrayed is not even the palest intimation of what is possible.

Did I believe that true connection might be possible with Bud? No, I did not. I wasn't hoping for it, either. As I said earlier, I was exhausted from the recent past, and I was allowing myself this convenient bit of exercise. Then again, I have been surprised more than once by what can occur when I let go of expectations. This evening, I expected little more than some enthusiastic pistoning leading to an easy climax. It would be enough – a sufficient diversion to hold back the onset of ennui.

When the hour arrived, Bud and I left quickly. He asked if I had a place nearby. I nodded. I had a midtown apartment I maintained for one of my out-of-town identities, a convenient and disposable safe-house. We walked the few blocks without talking. We both knew what we were up to, there was no need to negotiate. Once inside, we wasted little time removing our clothes.

The bow tie was a clip-on, his silk shirt unbuttoned smoothly – revealing an attractive, rugged body. His chest hair, dark and curly, formed a classic tree-of-life. He stretched his arms, his upper torso muscular, his shoulders and arms well-corded, but he moved with an easy grace, comfortable in his body. Levis dropped to the floor, revealing well-shaped legs and calves. His black silk boxers bulged with anticipation.

He pushed me backward onto the bed. I allowed it to happen. Normally, I am not the submissive partner, but tonight I was coasting, allowing events to proceed as they would. In contemporary terms, I am pansexual, I am whatever my partner wants me to be, so it was easy for me to lie back in anticipation of what this man intended.

He tugged off my briefs, studied me for barely an instant – I have always been slim, never truly muscular, and after my transformation, I have maintained an unusually youthful appearance. Young blood helps with that, the younger the better. I admit it is uncharacteristic, but I'm not yet ready to age. Older blood has more character, but younger blood has greater vitality, and I prefer the bounce it gives me.

But I wasn't looking at Bud that way. As I have said more than once, I am not a glutton, and I do not need to feed as often as portrayed in the movies. Once or twice a month is sufficient. And it isn't necessarily a fatal encounter for my selected partner. Only when – but I'm still getting to that.

Bud studied me for a moment. Compared to him, I was skinny, undeveloped. And because I was so slight and pale, perhaps he saw me as effeminate. That had always been part of my attraction to some of my patrons. And certainly, Bud had chosen me for some reason. He had flirted with me deliberately, and he had asked me to wait and meet him at midnight. He would not have done so had he not desired me –

So I expected Bud to be as affectionate in bed as he had been at the bar. I expected a slow sincere seduction. Instead –

He flung himself at me, straddling me like a cowboy on a steer and began slapping at my face and arms, the whole time shouting a stream of invective so startling, I didn't know whether to laugh or cry –

I cried.

What? You think Vampires have no souls, no feelings? We do. And so much more intensely than even the most passionate of daysiders –

Bud had caught me when I was vulnerable. When I was still feeling the pain and hurt of what I had previously lost. I had not yet expressed my grief, I was still carrying it around inside, like an oyster clutching the sandy irritant that would some day become a pearl, but for the moment was still a source of anguish. He'd caught me by surprise and my emotions burst from me in an explosion of sudden gasps and sobs. I had not known I was still so deep in my distress.

My tears must have excited him, because he now increased his efforts. Enraged, he kept slapping at my face, shrieking now –

"This is what you deserve, you ugly little piece of puke. This is what a real man does to a faggot like you –" And more. Much more, much worse. He used words I would not repeat anywhere. And the whole time, he pumped furiously at his organ. The greater his abuse, the greater his arousal.

I let him pummel me – for the moment, I wasn't afraid. In fact, I welcomed it. The stimulation of this beating was a purge, a scouring, a scourging of the horrible detritus of the despair that had crippled me for so many long weeks. So yes, I welcomed it. I encouraged it. I shrieked with pain – and yes, it hurt, but it was a delicious hurt –

And the whole time, part of my mind was wondering how this charming bartender had become the author of this monstrous assault. Was this his normal release? And if so, where did he find partners? And why hadn't anyone else at that bar warned me? Surely, someone else must have known this truth.

It was only when he started punching me that I realized the intensity, the depth of his fury. This wasn't just a sexual release for Bud – he intended to hurt me. His expression was distorted with rage, his mouth twisted, his eyes burning. This crazed man was strong enough to injure me and he was furious enough to do so. Despite my enhanced ability to heal, I began to fear the level of damage he could inflict. He might even need to kill me to achieve the emotional release he so desperately craved.

It was when he raised his fist too high – high enough to deliver a punishing blow – that my alarm finally exploded. With a burst of internal fire flooding outward from my heart, I flashed into Q-time, that acceleration of the flesh that turned the rest of the world into a slowed-down panorama. His fist came down slowly – slow enough for me to watch it in amusement – and sank deeply into the mattress beside me. I had already twisted away. Missing me, not meeting the expected resistance of my terrified face, put him off balance, he fell slowly sideways just enough that I could roll backward, bringing up my knee, my foot, to sink it into his solar plexus, pushing into it, pushing and pushing and pushing until he rose up and away, flying slowly, gracefully backward off the bed, arms spreading outward in surprise, astonishment creeping across his face, until he slammed against the ceiling – hard! Even in Q-time, I could feel the impact. He held there for a long slow-motion moment, then began descending as gently as a deflating balloon – by which time I had already rolled off the bed, sticking the landing like a champion gymnast.

I only look harmless. That's my power.

Bud splatted onto the bed, face-planting into the mattress, sprawling in shock, gasping, unable to breathe, barely able to curl himself into a ball around the horrible knot of pain in his gut. I had aimed my kick deliberately.

There's this about violence – as much as the movies lie about sex, they lie about fighting even more. In the real world, most fights are over quickly. In the movies, the opponents are always equally matched and equally indestructible, enduring assaults that would cripple a normal person.

In real life, the one with the power disables the target as quickly as possible, usually with a single, well-placed application of force to the most vulnerable part of his opponent's body. One good kick to the solar plexus – actually one exceptional kick – and it was enough to slam Bud into the ceiling above the bed. Hard enough to crack the ceiling plaster — and possibly his spine as well. After that, gravity did the rest.

By the time he was mostly through vomiting, Q-Time had eased, not completely, but enough that I could start to recover my own strength. I had my head low, my hands on my knees. I was gasping for breath as well – that sudden swift exertion of energy was going to cost me. I was good for another hour or two – after that, I'd need a few hours of dormancy. Four, maybe six.

I awoke to sunlight streaming in through a crack in the curtains. I was sprawled across the living room sofa. Judging by the angle of the sunbeams, it was late afternoon. I'd slept longer than I intended. And I still felt weak and groggy.

Coffee first. While it was brewing, I took a long hot shower. I ignored the muffled noises coming from the bedroom. Time enough for that later.

When I finally entered the bedroom, Bud's frantic eyes followed my every movement. He made some noises from behind the gag, but I ignored them. I did check the bindings on his arms and legs; they were secure. My long-dead father had taught me well – I still remembered how to tie a secure knot. It was the only legacy he'd left me, but I'd made good use of it more than once. This time, I had cut

Bud's black silk shirt into narrow strips, braided them for strength, and tied him spread-eagled to the four bedposts.

I dressed in silence; there was no need to talk to Bud. Not any more. He'd waived all rights the moment he curled his hand into a fist – the moment he'd decided to hurt me. First, I had some shopping to do.

It was late enough in the day that most of the streets were already shadowed. That's one of the advantages of living in a city of canyons. It's easy to avoid direct sunlight. I spread my purchases up the east side of Manhattan and down the west. There wasn't a lot I needed, but I didn't want to look suspicious, either.

By the time I got back, the sun had already set. I unpacked the shopping cart methodically, laying things out in neat rows on the table in the dining nook. Decisions, decisions. I started with the baby bottle. I filled it with milk and put it in a pan of water on the stove. A very low heat. While it warmed, I unwrapped the rest of the packages.

First, I lit the incense. Patchouli. A particularly noxious scent, but while it wouldn't blanket the most offensive odors, it would mask them enough to be tolerable.

Then, I filled a bowl with warm soapy water and dropped the bathing sponge into it. As I expected, when I entered the bedroom, Bud was a mess. He lay there in a puddle of his own urine and feces. He looked haggard. His eyes were wild. And even without asking, I could tell that his muscles were cramped with the effort of trying to break free. Not from my daddy's knots. His distress was palpable.

Without acknowledging his predicament, I began to quietly and methodically wash him. I lost count of how many times I had to empty the bowl into the toilet and refill it with clean water. But I didn't stop until the stink of shit and sweat and urine was no longer a visible haze in the air and the apartment reeked of patchouli.

At some point, I stripped the sheets and mattress pad from the bed and dropped them into the bathtub. I left them to soak in detergent overnight. I'd probably have to rinse and soak them several times. Eventually, I'd let them dry so I could send them out with the rest of the laundry. It wasn't the first time I'd done this. Fortunately, there was a rubber sheet on the bed, so the mattress would remain unsoiled.

Finally satisfied, I returned to the kitchen and washed my hands for several long minutes in water almost hot enough to scald. I had a lot on my mind. Had I forgotten anything?

I returned to the bedroom with the package of adult diapers. I didn't bother to explain to Bud the necessity. I could tell from his frantic expression that he understood – he was going to be here for a while. To his credit, he didn't struggle much – then again, I hadn't left him much wiggle room when I'd tied him down.

By now the milk was warm enough. I held up the bottle so he could see what I had. "This is it. This is all you're going to get. Nothing else." I sat down next to him on the bed.

"Now, before we start, I want you to understand something. From this moment on, you have only two choices. You can die painfully – or you can take a long time to die and you will die very painfully. It's up to you. If you understand, blink twice."

Blink. Blink.

"Next. You are not to talk to me. You are not to say anything at all. We are not ready to have a conversation. You have not earned the right to a conversation. You are entitled to silence, nothing else. If you understand, blink twice."

Blink. Blink.

"Good. Now, in a minute, I will remove the duct tape from your mouth. If you scream, if you speak, if you say anything at all, I'll put the tape back on and you will not get your dinner. If you understand, blink twice."

Blink. Blink.

"Good. Very good."

I held up the bottle so he could focus on it. "It's just milk. Warm milk. Just what every little baby boy wants. Do you want your bottle now?"

Blink. Blink.

I removed the duct tape slowly. The quick rip is more sudden and more painful, but the slow peel back is easier to replace if the person breaks his promise not to talk.

To his credit, Bud was very good at following instructions. He sucked at the nipple hungrily, gulping at the milk as fast as he could manage. When he finally finished, his eyes were wet with tears – either shame or gratitude, I couldn't tell and didn't care. I wiped his face with a clean towel, then applied a fresh piece of duct tape across his mouth.

Yes, we could have had a conversation. We could have had many conversations. But I didn't feel like it. I didn't see the point. You don't talk to your hamburger, do you? Besides, I knew all the variations already: "Why are you doing this to me?" "What do you want?" "I have money!" "Please, please, for the love of God, have some mercy!" "What kind of a monster are you?!" And all the other things they say – all the things that never work.

I picked up the blue blanket from the foot of the bed and pulled it over him, tucking him in carefully. I even laid my hand on his forehead and gave him a gentle kiss. The expression in his eyes was terrified. "Sleep tight, baby. Tomorrow is another day."

Yes, it would be. I hadn't put my hand on his forehead out of gentleness, I was checking his temperature. It was already dropping. He was right on schedule. By morning he'd be feverish and I'd have to connect the IV. He'd need a lot of nutrients to keep his strength up. I didn't want him to die. Not yet, anyway.

I wasn't happy that he was in my bed. I didn't like sleeping on the sofa. I could have gone back to my apartment in the village, but I didn't want to leave him alone and untended, either.

This whole project had been a spur of the moment decision, motivated more by anger than anything else. I had chosen it, so I had to live with the consequences. The sofa it was.

And I didn't like having my sleeping hours reversed either – he had me keeping the same hours as a daysider. I'd have to do something about that as quickly as possible.

I won't go into the details of Bud's transformation. It's really rather mundane. But I did finally remove the tape from his mouth so we could talk.

No, I didn't owe it to him. I didn't owe him anything, but I had grown bored waiting for him to ripen. His physical strength was sufficient to give him some resistance to the process, so I needed him to tell me what he was feeling, what physical sensations he was experiencing.

"That was a lucky kick," he said.

"If that's what you want to believe, okay." I continued placing ice packs on his chest and belly. "This should help with the burning. A little, anyway."

"I feel weird. What did you do to me?"

"Just a little – oh, let's call it seasoning – to improve the flavor."

"You drugged me."

"That's one way of saying it. Not very accurate, but –"

"Whatever you think you're doing, you won't get away with it."

"Mmm hmm. Someday, one of you fellows will be right about that."

That shut him up for a moment. The realization that he wasn't the first – and that I knew what I was doing.

"I'm sorry –" he said.

That stopped me. I put the last ice pack on his chest and didn't move for a long moment. I left my hand on his sternum, feeling the nervous beat of his heart beneath. Finally, I looked at his face. It was the first time I'd met his eyes since tying him to the bed.

No one had ever said that to me before. And by the twisted and distressed look of his features, I understood that he'd never said it to anyone either.

His voice cracked. "Please, I'm so sorry. I really am –"

"This is the first time you've ever apologized…?"

He hesitated, then finally admitted, "Yes…it is." His eyes were getting shiny, welling up with tears.

"Then, I'm not the first man you've ever beaten up, am I?"

"No."

"Can't you just have sex with a man?"

"It's not enough."

His response repelled me. I had no choice but to ask the next question. "How many…?"

He shook his head. "I don't know. I don't remember."

"How badly did you hurt them?"

He didn't answer. He couldn't.

"Did you kill anyone?"

Again, he shook his head – a denial, a refusal, a retreat.

"Did you kill anyone?" I demanded.

"I don't know. I don't think so. Maybe once. I don't know. I didn't wait to see. I never heard –"

"None of them ever went to the police?"

His voice broke, but he managed to get the words out anyway. "The cops don't care. They laugh. They'd say he deserved it for being a fag."

"But you're not –?"

"Naw, man. I'm not. I mean – I'm not."

"But you invite men to have sex with you –"

"But it's not sex –"

"If it's not sex, then what is it?"

"It's – it's what I do."

"Uh-huh. It's what you do. And yes, what you do is definitely not sex. It's something else. Something sick. Too bad you never learned how to have sex. Real sex. You wouldn't be here now – in this situation." I paused, studying him. He did have an attractive body. Spread-eagled like that, he was an open invitation. I allowed myself a delicious smile – enough to terrify him. "But maybe...just maybe, I'll show you what real sex is. Maybe – if the circumstances are right – I'll give you the chance to find out what real pleasure is."

A flicker of hope crossed his face – and fear as well.

"But not yet. You're not ready. Nowhere near –" I took my hand from his chest. "Are you hungry? Should I get you another bottle?"

"Please? Could I have something else instead? Real food?"

"No, you can't. You're still a baby. My baby. My sweet little baby boy. And we have a long way to go before I trust you enough to put anything solid in your mouth."

"I'm sorry." He tried again. "I'm really, really sorry."

"I know you are. And I forgive you. Now open your mouth, baby boy. If you want your ba-ba."

"Do I shock you, Joseph?"

"Uh-uh. I'm not tied down to the bed."

"Would you like to be?"

"No, thank you. I'm quite comfortable this way."

He laughs and my head bobbles with his amusement.

I'm resting my head on Jacob's cool chest, he has one arm around my shoulder. Occasionally, he strokes my back. The tingling has become fire, the burning flashes out in waves, but it's a good feeling now. I'm floating in the center of a starburst of sensation. Strange colors flicker at the edges of everything, and everywhere a crackling sense of something – I don't have words for it yet.

"But you have questions."

"You've done this before...?"

"Not as often as you want to assume. It's a lot of work."

"There are two of us now. I can help –"

Jacob laughs and my head bobs again. "I didn't imagine you would be impatient."

"I'm not impatient. It's just that there's so much to learn –"

"More than you know."

"Enough for another book?"

"Enough for a trilogy. Maybe a septology."

"I'll have time."

"You might not want to write it, my dear. It could be a very dangerous set of revelations –"

"If I was afraid of danger, I wouldn't be here."

"That's true," Jacob says. His voice softens, his hand rests firmly on my spine, listening, tasting. "How are you feeling?"

"How am I feeling?" I look inside, all the strangeness, the experience of stretching, expanding. Where are the words for this?

Finally, "I'm flying – I'm flying on a magic carpet – a delicious man-ride, a silver slither in the sky. The stars are flowering all around us. Such beautiful colors"

Jacob strokes my hair. "Are you hallucinating or just showing off your skill with linguistic allusions?"

"Yes...."

"I see."

"Am I there yet?"

"Not yet. But soon."

We rest in silence for a while. Starflakes of desire and apprehension surround me, all in shades of white and gold and rose. And a darker apprehension of hunger, as well.

Bud was strong, even stronger than he looked. His transition took the better part of a week. When the burning ebbed, he slipped deep into a dormant state, the cells of his flesh slowly regenerating into a different kind of existence.

By then, I was no longer feeding him milk. He was taking a bottle of rich beef blood every two hours. It's not that hard to obtain, not if you have a Companion working in a slaughterhouse. I could have gotten him human blood as well – but that was a luxury he didn't deserve.

Even before he resurrected – that's the Community's term for the first awakening, our own little ironic joke – even before he resurrected, I had already tapped the artery in his right arm. I'd taken a few sips, but like any vintage worth savoring, he needed time to mature.

When he finally awoke, the first thing he did was test his bonds. He struggled on the bed for a while, twisting and writhing until he realized it was useless. Finally, he looked up at me. "You changed them –?"

"I did. The silk was strong, but not strong enough. These are stronger."

"You're a son of a bitch –"

"You've already called me worse."

"I apologized."

"And I forgave you."

"Then why didn't you let me go?"

"Because I might have forgiven you, but all those others – they didn't. They trusted you, they took you to their beds, and you betrayed them. You beat them up. You might have crippled and maimed them. You hurt them – not just physically. You made them afraid. You made them afraid to love. I can forgive you, because I'm not them. But they can't forgive you – because you took something away from them that can never be recovered. You took away their willingness to trust. I don't think that part can be forgiven."

"You bastard –"

"Accident of birth," I said calmly. "But you – you had a choice. And this is what you chose."

He fell silent then, his expression said it all. If I had not strengthened his bonds, we could have had hours of glorious combat, a deliciously brutal mutual pummeling. But as arousing as some might find that, I do not. I have spent a century and a half avoiding serious discomfort. I have no taste for it. Perhaps if I had been possessed of a larger, more rugged physique, I would feel differently about the extremes of athleticism, but I am comfortable in my body – indeed, I'm actually quite fond of my appearance. I have even – when it has been convenient – been able to pass for a young woman, if one does not study me too closely. That is not one of my desires either. But I like the ability to be a wraith. It's a survival skill.

At last, he spoke again. This time, his voice was quieter. His fury subsided, he had descended into resignation and resentment. "What did you do to me?"

I sat down next to him on the bed. I touched his chest, put my hand on his heart to listen, to taste. "I seasoned you –"

"What the hell does that mean?"

"It means you didn't have enough flavor before. Now you do."

He hesitated, uncertain. I have to admit, my answer was designed to terrify him.

His eyes were wide now. "So...which is this?" he asked.

"Which is what?"

"You said I had a choice."

"Oh. Yes, I did."

"You said I could die painfully...or very painfully."

"No, I said you could take a long time to die – and die very painfully."

"I cooperated with you –"

"Yes, you did. That's why you get to take the long time to die – and very painfully. Very, very painfully. Because that was what you chose."

"No, I didn't – I didn't choose that."

"Yes, you did. And this is it. But if you're as smart as you pretend to be, which I like to think you are, you will enjoy dying very painfully a lot more than you would have enjoyed just dying."

"You're crazy."

"Yes, maybe. Certainly by your definition of sanity. Not by mine. Now, the real fun begins."

"This isn't fun for me –"

"No, it isn't. But you already had your fun, dear. Now, it's my turn." I made as if to rise, then turned back to him. "We could have had some fun together. If you had been that kind of man. And if you had been, you'd be back at work tonight. But I brought you up here to have some fun – and if I'm not going to have fun one way, then I'm going to have it another way. This is it. And if you're starting to feel just a little bit like some of the men you abused – well, consider that a bonus. You get to have fun their way now."

I got up and went to the kitchen, filled a bowl with warm soapy water, procured a towel and a sponge, and returned to the bedroom. "It's time for your bath, little boy –"

Yes, I was humiliating him. I was doing it deliberately. I wanted him angry, and I wanted him afraid. I wanted him in tears, as well. I wanted to reduce him to a completely infantile state – so that his fear and rage were complete and total and ferociously beyond his ability to control. I didn't need to hurry this – I needed to break him, shatter him into fragments, and leave what was left resigned to the reality that this was his existence. Nothing else.

After I cleaned him, I gave him a gentle dusting of baby powder so he'd smell good. I sat down next to him on the bed again. "I want you to notice something – you've been strapped down to this bed for the better part of a week. But you're not cramping up, you're not hurting, you're not getting weaker; if anything, your muscles are tighter than ever. You are, in one sense, in the best shape of your entire life.

"I want you to notice something else, as well. Your senses have been heightened. You can hear the rats scrabbling through the woodwork three floors below. You can see every speck of dust in the air illuminated by nothing more than distant starlight. You can smell the flavors coming from the restaurants two blocks away. And your sense of touch –? The nerves beneath your skin are flickering with impatience. You can taste the dancing moments of the breeze, all the seasons of life. You hunger for sensation –

"Close your eyes and look inside. You can feel the waves of blood pulsing outward from your heart, across your chest and belly, out through your arms, down through your legs, echoing off the extremities of fingers and toes, and bouncing back again to be recycled through your lungs. Feel your lungs expanding, tasting and savoring the air. Notice how your organs fit together, slide against each other. Feel the peristaltic churning of your intestines. Everything – notice all the different processes of the flesh, that's you – all of that is you, I want you to feel it intensely –

"No, don't resist. Resistance is pain. Experience it. Experience is sensation. When you let it in, you become it, it becomes you –"

No, I wasn't hypnotizing him, I was meditating him – and he interrupted it to ask, "Is this it? Is this when you give me my very painful death?"

If I had laughed, it would have terrified him. I did not, but yes – I found his reaction amusing. "No, I am not going to hurt you tonight. I'm going to do something worse. I'm going to give you pleasure – the most intense pleasure you have ever experienced in your short, pathetic life. Bud, my little baby, I am going to take you so far beyond the limits of ecstasy, so far past anything you could ever have imagined, that you will never again be satisfied with anything less."

That was the most terrifying thing I could have said. He didn't realize the full horror of it – if he had, he would have screamed for the mercy of instantaneous oblivion, but he recognized enough of it that his eyes widened in apprehension. And his heartbeat quickened – with both fear and eagerness.

"Are you ready to begin? Never mind, it doesn't matter. I'm ready –

"Let me tell you about the human body. Did you know I'm a doctor? I've been studying medicine for…oh, it must be seventy years now. We've made a lot of advances. And with tools like the new electron microscope, who knows what we'll discover about how human biology works? It's an exciting time to be alive. Another seventy years, we might even know how to assemble the fundamental chemicals of life – what miracles will we accomplish then? But you don't need to concern yourself with that question, you won't be around for that. I will, but you won't.

"Oh, but I was talking about the body today, wasn't I? And what we know about it right now, how it grows and develops, how it works. You see, dear little baby boy – we all start out as girls. Every single one of us. Still with me? It's about to get exciting –"

Bud's attention was on my face, on my voice. He was so caught up in the word pictures I'd been painting, he hadn't noticed that my fingers had been circling out from his heart, tracing patterns around the left side of his chest, and now – only now, slowly narrowing in on the target.

I leaned forward then, putting myself directly in his line of sight, just close enough for him to focus on my eyes. "Let me tell you how you got here, baby boy. It's an amazing journey. Your daddy – he put his penis inside your mommy, back and forth, back and forth, in and out, in and out – he probably thought he was having fun, maybe even the most fun a man can have – well, what passes for fun for men like that. Two or three minutes, maybe five – and then bam! A few quick spurts and it was all over – maybe it felt like a big thing to him, but if he was like most men, doing it the way most men do, it wasn't anywhere near what it could have been. That spurt contained a few million little swimmers, and one of those swimmers – the fastest one or the strongest one – well, that little swimmer got to the egg, and well – despite all the odds against it, you got started. There were a million other little swimmers, a million other little people who could have gotten started, but you got here. Isn't that amazing?

"Now...for the first eight weeks, just floating inside mommy's safe little space, you were just a funny-looking little pink salamander, as sexless as a jellybean. Not much to look at, really. But as I said, after a couple months, if you've got boy chromosomes, something inside the jellybean lets loose a little squirt of boy-juice, and that causes the tiny little button at the bottom end of your notochord, what will eventually be your spinal cord, to become a pee-pee. Isn't that interesting?

"Never mind, we're not interested in your little pee-pee yet. See, until that little squirt of boy-juice, you're still a girl. Well, developing like one. And that's why, when you finally pop out of mommy's warm oven, you have these two little reminders that you were once a little girl – these cute little nipples right here. This one and this one. Because they started developing before that little squirt of boy-juice gave you a pee-pee. Yes, it's such a cute little pee-pee – and because it's the bottom end of your spinal cord, you think it means something. As soon as you can get your fat little hand into your diaper, wrapping your pudgy little fingers around it, you decide it's important. Silly you. But these other two things, right here, where you can see them every time you take off your shirt, every time you look in the mirror, these rosy little peaks – you think they're useless? Oh, no. They're there to remind you that inside, you've got some girl stuff. A lot of girl stuff. I'll let you in on a secret. These two little peaks, they're really little volcanoes just waiting to erupt –"

I pinched his left nipple hard enough to make him flinch. "See? Just like a girl – a very girly-girl – you've got a lot of very active nerve-endings inside there. Most men don't realize it, you probably didn't think much about it – but your nipples are very, very sensitive. And yours – more so now than ever before. You can feel everything." I squeezed again. "See? And this is the part where it finally gets really, really exciting –"

By now, I'd been tracing circles around the left areola long enough that it must have been getting very sensitive – almost raw.

And every so often, I'd give it a pinch or a tweak – or I'd roll the roseate flesh between my fingers. I needed to keep all the nerves firing.

When I finally felt enough heat beneath my fingers, I leaned in and slowly licked his nipple, flicking it with my tongue.

He gasped –

That's when I began to suck it. Not ferociously, but sweetly, like an infant, like a lover, like an exquisite torturer, all of these at once.

Among the books I had in my library – in the locked part of my library – I had a shelf of rare and valuable volumes that had been imported at great expense from India, Japan and China. The illustrations were marvelous. All of the books were accompanied by painstakingly accurate English translations. Apparently, our far eastern cousins had been studying the intricacies of the human body for millennia, much longer than any western practitioners.

Some of the books were about the methodologies of torture. Others were about the physics of sexual congress. The two subjects were not that far apart – both were about the repertoire of stimuli available to the human body and ways to evoke specific suites of sensation. Over the years, I'd had opportunities to practice many of these techniques. Tonight, however, I had a specific goal in mind.

It is not commonly known – indeed, I would not have known it had I not experienced it myself – but you can bring even the most rugged man to orgasm merely by sucking his nipple. It takes time and intention, it requires patience and cooperation, and it is not a male orgasm, that sudden explosion of sexual energy – it is a female response, a gradual ascension of pleasure, culminating in waves of delight and joy. I had time. I had patience. There was no need to hurry. I intended to enjoy myself.

Poor Bud had no choice but to lie back and let me have my way with his baby-smooth chest and his singularly exposed anatomy.

Oh, did I forget to mention? While he had been dormant, unable to move but still feeling everything in exquisite detail, I had shaved him clean and hairless. He had a magnificent body, even more so without those curly black mats everywhere. With his skin glistening all pink and shiny, he looked like he was sculpted out of exquisitely radiant porcelain. He almost looked like the innocent and beautiful teenager who might once have had a future. I think that may have been one of the reasons I intended to take such care with him. After everything he must have been through to turn him into what he became, he deserved the opportunity to be something else for a while.

By the time I had him moaning, even writhing in ecstasy, I knew that he had gone to that place where pain and pleasure were no longer identifiable as separate sensations. I could feel the physicality of sweetness flashing through his body, racing outward in waves of delight that ebbed only when I pulled back to survey the landscape of his rapture. I bent again to coax him to even greater peaks of emotion, and the intensity of his experience had him gasping, crying, even screaming in wordless grunts. I'd simultaneously raised him to the peak of sexual energy and reduced him to the basest level of animal existence.

After that, the rest was…well, even more fun. For both of us. I made sure of that. If even a single nipple can be an avenue to nirvanic bliss, it is almost beyond imagination what ecstasies are possible elsewhere in the human physiology. You think it's all about some specific erogenous zone? What foolishness. The entire human body is an erogenous zone.

Never mind. If you haven't been there, you haven't been there.

Within days, I had poor Bud begging for my attentions. I took him every way it is possible for one man to take another, and each time, I took him farther than the time before – until I had him passing out in delirious joy, and then coming back to consciousness with only a single, desperate plea on his lips. "More…more… Please, more. God, yes."

The physical bindings were long gone, unnecessary. He came crawling across the bed, naked, unashamed, begging for even the slightest touch of my hand. His body enflamed by the strange new blood coursing through his veins, he existed in a state of insatiable desire. He was consumed by it.

I had addicted him. Not hard to do, given his transformed physical state and the hallucinogenic mental processes that followed. I'd vampirized him, I'd stripped him of his humanity, and I'd overpowered his ability to experience his own body. I'd overwhelmed his soul.

From time to time, I tasted him, just the slightest sip. He didn't mind – he enjoyed it. For him, it was another way to experience pleasure. For me, however, it was the tasting of the dish as it simmered on the stove.

Bud's flavor was developing nicely. He was young and powerful, brutal and delicious. The aspects of desire were already creating in him a most savory vintage. He was going to be delicious. But it was still too soon. He wasn't ready yet. There was more to do. A great deal more.

I come awake, blinking. Jacob is watching, an impish smile in his eyes. "How are you feeling?"

"Amazed. I think that's the word for it."

"It's as good as any."

I turn on the bed to face him. "I thought that being dormant was supposed to be like death –"

He touches my cheek. His hand is cool and reassuring. "It can be. But it doesn't have to be. Sometimes you keep yourself awake and aware while you regenerate your strength. It takes longer, sometimes a lot longer, but when you're dormant, you're vulnerable. So sometimes, you only go part way down."

"It was weird. Even with my eyes closed, I was aware of everything around me. Like a dream –"

"It's called dreamtime. You'll learn to manage it. It takes practice. The first few times, when you're still learning how deep you can go, it can be kind of scary. It scared me. I thought I was dying. That's what it feels like. I came out of it screaming. But Monsieur was there to reassure me. No matter how deep you think you're going, you can't die in dreamtime. It doesn't work like that. Once you get some sense of your control, you'll see that you can go as deep as you want. One day you'll get curious how far down the bottom is – you'll find out there is no bottom. You'll see.

"Monsieur once showed me he could go dormant for weeks at a time. I expect that's one way to survive during times of famine. And that's probably how the whole undead mythology started, way back in times of superstition and ignorance. If you got infected back then, back before we learned how to be Nightsiders, you wouldn't really know what you were, would you? Think about it. If all a man knew were the horror stories of the dead rising from their coffins, given the hallucinogenic quality of the whole experience, it might have been enough to drive him into a waking madness. Maybe he'd believe he'd become some kind of undead thing, while at the same time, he'd be caught up in the extreme sensations and hungers of this new afterlife. I think that's how a lot of the mythology started. It would certainly be worth some serious study."

"If there were any records, yes –"

"Oh, there are. Church records, especially. But most of them are inaccessible. Locked up in the Vatican or buried in vaults somewhere. It wasn't exactly a popular subject. Monsieur knew quite a bit about it –"

"He was that old?"

"No. But his…his creator was. Or his creator's creator. I was never quite sure."

"Is that what you are? My creator?"

"That's one term for it. Patron or mentor are good words, too. It's whatever you want the relationship to be."

"Not master?"

"Nightsiders have no masters."

I rolled over and stared at the dog head on the ceiling. "Well, I'm kinda thinking…partner. Or lover."

"Too soon for that, sweetheart. Let's go with companion for now. Associate."

"Friend?"

"Mmm. Vampires don't have friends, either."

"We don't?"

"I haven't told you the rest of it. Then maybe you'll understand."

It did not take long. Within two weeks of that first seduction, Bud was completely enslaved by his own hallucinogenic desires. When he complained about having nothing to wear but diapers, I gave him a boon. We discarded the diapers in favor of frilly pink panties and a matching top, what they called a Baby Doll nightie. Bud was delighted at the silky sensations against his skin. He barely noticed the intentional humiliation of the circumstance – he was too consumed with the privilege of being a sissy-boy.

I'd done my job well. I'd managed his hallucinations from the beginning, regularly working his skin to keep it as sensitive as a newborn's. I now had him so terrified of the world beyond the bedroom that I could release him from his bonds and let him roam freely from one corner of the bed to the other. He was so whipped by his condition that he wouldn't use the bathroom unless I accompanied him to confirm that he was behaving like a good boy.

Eventually, he did overcome that reluctance when I showed him how much fun we could have in the shower and the bathtub. That became his second playroom, and he'd ask me every day if we could take a shower together, and if he was really, really a good boy, would I let him do this one thing he had learned to enjoy – or perhaps that other thing that he liked even more – or perhaps first one and then the other…?

And then, finally, on the day that even a slab of raw beef and a tumbler of beef blood were no longer enough to satisfy his physical hunger – on that day, it was time.

"I'm going to have to punish you, Bud –"

He leapt onto the bed eagerly, squirming in anticipation. He went down on his hands and knees and pushed his panty-clad butt up for the desired spanking. He wiggled his ass excitedly, an enthusiastic invitation – a hopeful provocation to the expected pleasures of epidermal assault and intestinal penetration.

Tempting, but no.

But we'd come so far in so few days. I had to smile.

Bud's disappearance from the bar had created a small stir among the patrons. I had slipped in quietly to see if he had been missed. Apparently, he had been a popular host and several of the patrons had expressed a flicker of regret before waving their glass for a refill. But the turnover in that community was fast-paced, and Bud had been quickly forgotten, his successor even more popular – and probably less dangerous to the clientele.

If they could have seen what he had turned into, scrambling around like a big clumsy puppy, a naked boy in rosy lingerie – they would have been shocked and embarrassed and disturbed. That was then – today, it would be an internet event, a viral sensation. The human race, ever inventive, has always found ways to turn its fetishes into commodities.

But it's unsurprising to a Nightsider.

It would be unsurprising to anyone who has journeyed through enough decades to see that the only thing that changes is the rationalization. Civilization is a pretentious justification. It's never been much more than a thin veneer laid over the squalid truth of a much darker nature. We are gluttons for sensation.

The difference between Nightsiders and daysiders is not our appetites – we share the same compulsions. No, the difference is that Nightsiders don't pretend to be good. We don't pretend to be sane. With the clarity of sense that comes with transformation, we know exactly what we are.

We are monsters, yes – but we know we are monsters. It is our choice to be monsters. We move among the daysiders, mostly undetected because we choose to remain undetected – and when we behave monstrously, it is also because we have chosen to do so.

Daysiders – the pathetic and unformed, the desperate and defeated – daysiders act as if they have no choice in the matter. That is why they are always so shocked when one or another of them is caught in monstrous behavior.

The difference? Nightsiders don't get caught.

I turned my attention back to Bud, still waggling his ass suggestively. "Please, sir. May I be punished?"

"Yes, you may – but not like that."

"How then, master –?"

"I'm going to tie you up again."

"With the ropes? Oh, yes. Please. Tie them tightly. Stretch me hard. I like that."

"You like everything now –"

"Because I can feel everything. Everything feels so good now. You taught me well. Please teach me some more."

Did the thought cross my mind that I might have gone too far with poor Bud, transforming him into such a pathetic figure, a sexual mendicant, a caricature of lust? Yes, the thought did occur to me – a pale echo of the moral sense my distant father had once tried to instill in my youthful soul. But I had only to remember Bud's own brutal behavior – his intention to punish me – to remind myself that what I intended next was an appropriate response. Appropriate for a Nightsider, that is.

"You're going to have to stand up for this one, Bud."

He looked puzzled, but complied.

"Now, you're going to have to take off your panties. And your bra."

I waited while he quickly scrambled out of them.

"Now, cross your arms over your chest – like this. That's it."

From the play chest at the foot of the bed, the chest I always kept locked, I took out several long rolls of gauze bandages and began wrapping them around his torso, pinning his arms to his chest. I wound the strips from his neck to his hips, then back up to his neck again, around and around, turning him slowly as I wrapped, until the upper half of his body was thoroughly mummified. A second set of rolls, and I bound his thighs and calves as well. I left his ass uncovered, his penis as well.

When I was done, I pushed him down onto the bed, centering him in the sheets, and tied him again so he couldn't roll away, not to the right, not to the left.

The whole time, he giggled in delicious anticipation, occasionally asking what I intended. I shook my head as I worked. "It's going to be the biggest surprise of all." Another few rolls for his head and his neck. I left his eyes and his mouth uncovered – as well as an access to his carotid.

When I was satisfied that he would not be able to free himself, I stepped back to survey what I had accomplished. I had reduced a dayside monster to a creature of nightside obsession. His obsession, not mine.

Nightsiders do not experience passion as an uncontrollable force, but as a store of energy to be appropriately channeled and focused as the need arises. Passion is a choice. Myself – I am passionate about my intentions, but I rarely dramatize them. Drama betrays the soul to others. Unchecked rage reveals where you hurt and where you can be hurt even worse.

Survival requires a veneer of impassivity, a seemingly dispassionate demeanor. From there, everything is deliberate, everything is a performance suited to the moment. That's a lesson that takes time to learn, even more time to put into practice – but everything I had done to Bud was the cumulative result of that education. And the end result – it was an expression of the highest art a Nightsider might aspire to, a symphony of emotional experience, a palette of exquisite sensations to be savored like wine.

From Bud's position, however –

Well, the trap had closed around him the moment he drew his arm back and curled his fist. From that moment, this was inevitable. But this is the part that neither Bud nor any other daysider could understand – nothing of what I had done was for the purpose of either his elevation or his embarrassment. None of it was about his experience at all. No – the entire process was merely a means to an end.

I sat down on the bed next to him. I put my hand on his heart. It was beating rapidly. He was delirious with anticipation. A multitude of sensations were piling up inside him – the feeling of the gauze against his skin, the tightness of his bindings, his inability to move, the complete loss of physical mobility, and the concomitant surrender to circumstance – his willing submission to my absolute control over his existence, all because of his addiction to the pleasures attendant to transformation. All of it was the deliberate and methodical progress toward this specific moment.

As I tightened the ball-gag so he could not speak, I patted him gently on the head, stroking him to ease his excitement and prepare him for what would come next.

"Do you remember when I said you could choose how to die? Painfully? Or very painfully? For a long time? Remember that? And you chose the long time and very painfully?"

He tried to nod. He couldn't. So he blinked twice.

"Well, this is that. This is where it begins. I taught you how to enjoy yourself. I want you to enjoy the exquisite pain that begins now."

His heart began beating faster with anticipation.

"One last thing. I'm going to leave you now. Will I be back? Maybe. Maybe not. You have no way of knowing, do you? So there is only one thing you can do – the only thing you are capable of now. You can go dormant. You can go deep. Just how long you survive will depend on how deep you go. I recommend going all the way down. There is no bottom, but go all the way anyway."

I started to rise, then stopped myself. I sat back down. "Nobody knows how long it's possible to stay down. The longest I've ever heard of anyone surviving was just a little over a century. But you're not really asleep. You're still kind of conscious the whole time. The one who stayed down for a century – when he came back up, he was insane. Of course, he'd been in a coffin that whole time, so that might have had something to do with it.

"I considered that for you – but it seemed like an awful lot of trouble, more effort than you really deserve. I think this will be more interesting for you – and more interesting for me in the long run. If I get curious, I might come back. But then again, maybe not. You weren't as interesting as I had hoped. And your flavor is – well, it's enthusiastic, but I doubt you'll ever be a treasured vintage, one worth aging in the cask, so to speak. But I could be wrong. Winemaking is a skill I haven't really mastered yet. I'm not sure anyone has – not this kind of liqueur, anyway."

I patted him on the head one more time, a gentle farewell. I locked the door on my way out.

"And you never went back?"

"On the contrary. Do you think I'm some kind of monster?" Jacob strokes my cheek, laughing gently. "Well, I am, yes – but I'm not that kind of monster."

"Huh?"

He leans over and kisses me. "You are so sweet. This is the part I love best. Shocking the newborn out of their naiveté."

"You're mocking me, aren't you?"

"Only a little."

"I know I'm not the first, but –"

"But you're the first in a long time who's gotten this far."

"You do realize, none of this is reassuring me –?"

"Joseph, my dear little sweetmeat. If I wanted you that way, I would have taken you that way a long time ago. And if you had wanted to escape this possibility, you would have been gone a long time ago. You can still walk out any time you want – but you won't, because you want to know the rest. You want it all. That's been clear from the beginning. No, my little morsel, I never had to stalk you. From the beginning, you set yourself out as bait for me."

I have no response to that. He's right.

"You pretended to be horrified, but you were fascinated. You pretended to be repelled, but you never realized how deeply I could read your reactions – you weren't casually attracted, you weren't enthusiastically interested – you were compelled to follow this journey to this end. You made yourself into something that you believed I would desire."

I can only nod in submission.

"I'm right, aren't I? Admit it."

"You're using the voice on me, aren't you?"

"No, I'm not. Admit it, Joseph. This is what you wanted from the beginning."

Hesitation. I understand the feeling. If I say yes, if I admit the truth – then I am finally, completely, totally, one with him. I will never be able to say he forced me into this, that I was unwilling…

If I say it, if I say the words, I will be crossing the final line.

"Is this what's different – between me and him? Me and the others?"

"If you say so, yes. If you choose it, yes." His eyes meet mine, his gaze is piercing. "Say it. Say the truth, Joseph."

"The truth…is…that yes, I did choose you. I chose this."

"Yes, you did." He puts a finger under my chin and lifts my face to his. "The truth about seduction – the truth about the submissive partner – it's the submissive who's in control. Nothing happens without the submissive's consent. He can say stop at any time – and it stops. Otherwise, it's rape. So he's really saying go, but go slow. Make it a delicate game of pretend-conquest, one nipple at a time."

Hmm.

"Think about it, Joseph. The submissive chooses it, every step of the way. I didn't seduce you, Joseph. You seduced me – it was all a dance of desire from the very beginning. You wanted me to seduce you, but it was you who opened the door and invited me in. Look inside – at your own feelings. Do you recognize that now?"

I blink hard. The truth is inescapable. Painful tears start to well up in my eyes.

"You see it now, don't you?"

I give him my humblest agreement. "That first night – when we went out in the dark, just to talk – whatever it was, yes, I felt something. And I wanted to know what it was I was feeling. I wanted – I didn't know what I wanted, I just knew I wanted it. Otherwise, I wouldn't have gone. Call it curiosity, attraction, even desire – but you must have sensed it. How could you not?"

"I saw what you were feeling…."

"So now you have to admit something too, Jacob – there was something about me that you wanted. Otherwise, I'd have never seen you again –"

"Yes, there was something. There still is."

"So, I got something right –?"

"More than something."

"Okay. Tell me. Why me? Why did you choose me? Or whatever – why did you let me choose you?"

"It was your curiosity as much as anything. No – that's not it. You wanted to learn, but more than that, it's that other thing you do – research. That was me when I started. Joseph, you're a scholar. And a reporter –"

"Oh, I'm a reporter? I reported your stories. Does that make me Dr. Watson?"

"My stories are true."

"So, I'm Boswell –"

"But you're telling your story, too."

"Ahh, I'm Proust."

"Oh, please no. You smell one silly cookie and it unleashes a whole torrent of memory, seven volumes and more, your whole tedious life story. What a ghastly bore – no, that's not you. You have enough skill to get to the punch line before I die of boredom."

"And what's the punch line here, my beautiful naked vampire man-boy…?"

"Ahh." Jacob sat up in bed, crossing his legs and facing me. "The punch line…?"

Bud wasn't very smart, he still thought he was playing his part in an intricate sex game – just another exquisite expression of his sexual enslavement. He never realized just how wrong he was – but he was smart enough to go dormant.

In fact, he went so dormant he didn't even wake up when I came back for my first taste – three weeks later, or maybe it was five or six weeks, I don't remember, and it doesn't matter.

I sat down on the bed next to him. I stroked his neck for a while. Finally I nipped at his neck, not a huge bite, just a little sip. He was developing well enough that I could wait a while longer to see what other flavors might express themselves.

It is in my nature to talk a subject to death. It is perhaps something I learned from Monsieur – first you explore and discover, you ask the first question and then you ask all the questions that are unlocked by that first one. And then, as you proceed deeper and deeper into that inquiry, you share what you are discovering so that it does not die with you. Sharing your journeys make them real – to yourself and to the people you share them with.

Sitting there next to him, listening to the darkness, the quiet grumbling of the sleeping city, watching the moonlight slowly cross the floor, I realized I was finally slipping back into my own contemplative state – that place of awareness without action, thought without intention – that sublime condition which defines the Nightsider existence. It is the ability to stand on the mountaintop of – oh, call it enlightenment, though it's anything but – and survey the entire landscape of existence spread out below as a feast to be enjoyed at leisure.

The thought did occur to me then that Bud and I did have a relationship, even though his perception of it was vastly different than my own, but because that relationship did exist – well, the performance of it anyway – I was duty bound to give him some explanation for what I had done to him – and why. If I did not explain it to him, then his side of the relationship would remain unresolved. And while another Nightsider might have taken a certain sociopathic delight in leaving Bud confused and alone, uncertain and hurting, silently traumatized by the apparent abandonment of his master – that was not me. I would have felt equally unresolved.

Let me clarify something here.

Two months had passed since that first night in June, Japan had surrendered and the nation had succumbed to its own delirium. No one knew what would happen next, but everyone was certain it would be wonderful. It probably would not be wonderful – the problems of cleaning up afterward are always much more complex than anyone considers while making the mess, and this is exponentially true of war – or any kind of violence.

But for a Nightsider, any dramatic shift in the national mood represents a wealth of opportunities – not just a marvelously enhanced menu at the buffet of humanity, but more than that, the chance to create new identities as insurance for long-term survival. As I have said before, a Nightsider must move at least once a decade, and usually more often than that.

Given all that, my obligation to the completion of Bud was significantly reduced. Indeed, I had no emotional investment in punishing him. He was just another piece of meat.

I could have taken him on that first night – but as I admitted at the beginning, I was bored. Worse than bored. I had been sinking into a languorous ennui.

Bud had been an opportunity to break that continuing decline in my spirits. Now that I had returned to the far more meditative state of Nightsider existence, my interest in Bud was significantly reduced. The exercise was in its final stages and my concerns would shortly be turning to the larger opportunities of the post-war situation.

Ultimately, I decided that it could be a useful opportunity to give Bud the truth of his situation – what would this new set of realizations and consequent emotions do to his flavor? Would it add delicious undertones of resignation and despair? Was he so enraptured by his submission to the inevitable that new flavors of joy and sweetness might develop? Or would he develop a rich blend of both at once? It was an interesting conundrum to consider. What could I say or do here that would achieve that combination of tastes?

By the time that train of thought had arrived at its terminus, I had been sitting with Bud, my hand resting on his chest, for more than an hour.

He was down deep, too deep to wake up easily, and I doubted he could learn how to come back up from that deep – not without a mentor. If I chose to leave him dormant, it might very well turn out to be a permanent slumber for him.

"So, Bud – here we are again. I know you can hear me. And I know you are wondering if you should wake up, but I don't think you know how and I'm not going to teach you, not tonight anyway. I think you should stay where you are. So just relax – well, you can't do anything else but relax – so that's all right. Just relax and listen.

"I suppose you're wondering when the fun begins. Well, this is it. This is the fun. Not yours. Mine. And for no reason at all that concerns you, I shall explain exactly why it is fun – for me. And maybe for you as well. If that's what you want.

"You see...this condition you're in now, way down there in that dark place of dream-time, this slowed-down time of geological awareness, it's not an unpleasant place to be – well, not unless you start to resist it. Then, it gets very unpleasant, very fast, and stays that way for a very long time. You can scare yourself to death that way. A long excruciating descent into madness – maybe followed by death, but probably not. I don't recommend it. So...because you really don't have a choice in anything that's going to happen for the rest of your life, your only option is to just let it happen. Relax. Submit. Surrender. And enjoy your long slow painful decline, into madness or death, your choice. There are many who would envy you. They never got that choice.

"Anyway – whatever you choose, this is the part where you die very painfully and take a long time doing it – whether you enjoy it or not. And now, I'm going to tell you the rest of it – so you can understand exactly why you have been given this particular ecstasy. Consider it a – oh, let's call it a boon, a favor, a gift. Because normally, I wouldn't bother. I mean, do you ever apologize to a pig for liking bacon...?

"You see, my little brute-sissy. There was something you asked once – way back when we started. You asked me why I was doing this, and I told you why. You had your fun. Now, it was my turn. It's still my turn. In fact, it has always been my turn.

"But don't take it personally. It was just – are you familiar with the word *karma*? It's an eastern concept. It's about how your actions make ripples in the world and those ripples come back to you – a fancy way of saying 'what goes around comes around.' What happened was you got what you created. I was just the...um, what's a good word...the instrument of delivery.

"You see, when we got into this bed – remember that? I thought we were going to have some fun together. But we didn't. I mean, you had fun – but it wasn't fun for me. Remember? You hit me. You slapped me. You called me names. You raised your fist to me. You treated me like an object for your selfish gratification – do you remember that? It seems like such a long time ago, doesn't it? But that was when you chose this. Because that was the moment that I chose you as an object for my selfish gratification. Fair is fair, correct? Of course, my gratification takes a lot more effort than yours..."

I stroked his chest lightly. Even through his bandages, all those layers of gauze wrapping, the sensation must have been marvelous and excruciating. His eyes flickered, but didn't open. He was so deep he was cold. Room temperature. When they found him – well, it would probably be an interesting autopsy – especially when the first knife went in and he came screaming awake. Pity the poor pathologist.

"Y'know, Bud – this is only vaguely relevant, but maybe it isn't. It seems to me sometimes that people like you tend to channel yourselves into specific patterns of conduct. The obvious example of course is the dominant-submissive structure of sexual gratification. It's a binary construct, Bud – apparently limited only to black and white, with no real shades of gray between. You are either one or the other, a top or a bottom – so when a person is limited to that way of thinking, he becomes self-limited to only two possible roles. Top or bottom. Dominant or submissive. That's not me, I find that boring – but apparently that was all you were capable of, wasn't it?

"Maybe you believed you were a dominant. And maybe you needed to express it as brutality. But I think there's more to it than that. I think you were ashamed of your own desires – and therefore you had to punish anyone who saw you as desirable that way. You would be an interesting chapter in any textbook on psychology.

"Anyway, if that was your sexual identity – and based on the evidence of the past two months, I think I'm right about this – when that specific expression was taken away from you, completely and totally obliterated as an option, there was no place for your identity to go, was there? No escape, except to assume the reverse expression of that same role. You flipped over completely and became the most abject submissive. And my dear sweet puppy, apparently, you have been enjoying it even more than your time as a dominant. This seems to have been what you wanted all along – someone to force you into your own desires, so you wouldn't have to be ashamed of enjoying them. You can still pretend it wasn't your choice. Except – well, in this case it was. Remember? I gave you the choice.

"Okay, I admit it – I wasn't completely honest. But then again, neither were you in your invitation, so let's not worry about which of us is the bigger monster or who was the most at fault. It doesn't matter. This collision was inevitable the moment you raised your fist to me.

"You do know what I am, don't you? You must have figured it out by now. And you must also have realized what I turned you into – oh, wait." I lifted my hand away from his chest, I held it up in mock denial – an unnecessary gesture to be sure, but I was beginning to feel melodramatic.

"Yes, I turned you. I created you. I transformed you – but despite that, you are nothing like me. Nothing at all. And you never will be. That was never a possibility. You are not my equal, you will never be my equal.

"You, my dear – you are a snack table. Maybe, with a bit of thyme and seasoning, you could become a whole meal – but right now, you're still a snack.

"But then, you should have realized that by now. All the sipping and tasting I've been doing – like an Italian grandmother fussing over the sauce –

"Let me explain. I get hungry. Approximately once a month. No, not the full moon. The dark of the moon. I don't need a whole meal, but I do need to slake my thirst – enough to satisfy the cravings that arise. And over time, I have become something of a connoisseur. It was inevitable. Doing the same thing over and over – first it's a habit, then it's a routine, finally it's a rut. And a rut is a grave with the ends knocked out. So…I look for variation. And over time, my tastes have become more than epicurean – they have become esoteric and exotic. You – don't flatter yourself – are nowhere near the pinnacle of taste. But you are – well, you are what you are – a demonstration that even a casual slab of flank steak can be tasty with the right preparation.

"The goal in any project of this type is to create a unique vintage. To an ordinary human being, one who has not been given this particular gift, blood is blood, it all tastes the same – a little salty, a little metallic, a little meaty. But to a Nightsider, blood is nectar and this is the important part, every person has a unique flavor – a distinctly identifiable blend.

"Pay attention now, Bud. This is important. Someone who has lived a reckless life, too much of this and too much of that, he's overspiced – he's a Texican burrito loaded with jalapenos and habaneros and God knows what else – not my style, very much an acquired taste. On the other hand, a teenager, young, and naïve and mostly inexperienced – that's a nice healthy drink, youthful blood is invigorating, but too often it's as flavorless as veal, occasionally delicious, but just as often as unsatisfying as oatmeal. Now, if you can find an innocent lover, blood laden with endorphins – he can be as sweet as peppermint ice cream, but cloying.

"When you've been around for a while – half a century or more – sampling here, sampling there, occasionally gorging, you begin to develop a sense of taste. The more you drink, the more that taste develops. What do they say? Taste is the product of a thousand distastes? That's even truer for a Nightsider. A quickie grabbed in a dark alley is little better than the grilled hockey puck they call a hamburger at the Woolworth lunch counter. Frankly, my dear – I do not want an industrial burger. I want prime rib.

"And…when I can have it, when I can make it myself, that's when it's the best. Are you getting it yet? The darkest blood is the richest. And the richest blood is vampire blood. I wish you could taste yourself.

"The blood of the Nightsider is the best. It has the most subtle of flavors, deep and rich, unfolding on the tongue like a symphony. What makes it so delicious and desirable is a marvelous symphony of flavor. It's the seasonings, the spices of emotion and experience, all of them together – as carefully blended as fine whiskey, aged for decades in an oaken cask. That was why I turned you, Bud. For the flavor."

Was that a flutter of emotion? It was too faint even for me to tell. I could have taken a sip, but if the emotion had been that faint, the flavor would have been undetectable. Never mind.

I patted his chest and went on. "But even fresh vampire blood – like yours now – has a youthful and intoxicating quality. You see, the real flavor of the vintage develops in the fermenting – the process of transformation.

"A good transformation takes time – not just the physical process, but all the learning that must come afterward as well. That's the best vintage. But – if you're like me, occasionally impatient, and if you're hungry enough and if it's obvious that all you have is hamburger, not prime rib – then you settle for a well-prepared burger. It depends on the Nightsider. And like everything else, it's a matter of taste. I'm not boring you, am I?"

I laid my hand back on Bud's chest. His heartbeat remained glacial, counting out his dreamtime in a funereal beat. Not even a flutter.

"All right, Bud, I will admit – in the beginning, in that first moment of capture, yes, you had some flavor, a strong flavor, but a very simple flavor, lacking any real depth. And frankly, it had very little potential.

"But I was bored. Bored enough to be curious. Bored enough to experiment – what might be possible with a little seasoning, a little spice? You see, what you were missing was the full range of human emotion, and I began to wonder what you might taste like with a modicum of Nightsider flavor added. That would require some effort on my part, but at the time, like I said, I was bored, and I was curious, and I had nothing else to do.

"Oh, I won't pretend I didn't enjoy the exercise. I enjoyed it quite a bit. Humiliating you, Bud – humbling you, reducing you to the most abject of all submissive behaviors – there was a poetic satisfaction to it. You confirmed my belief about the binary character of your sexual identity – indeed, the shift in your behavior occurred so quickly you surprised me. Thank you for that. There is little that surprises me anymore.

"And yes, you seasoned up well – better than I expected, although not quite as flavorful as I had hoped. But that's not my fault. It's yours. You're really quite a shallow fellow.

"Nevertheless, it was worth the effort. I took you through as much of the emotional landscape as you were capable of expressing. Fear? That's where I started – fear is the fundamental ground of being for anything with a spinal cord. What's that lurking in the dark? What just made that noise? What's out there? And what's going to happen to me? Oh yes, Bud, I had you nervous, I had you queasy – but most of all, I had you panicked, terrified, pissing your diaper in fear. That frozen chill of terror – your sweat reeked of it. Your heart beat so fast you were in danger of a cardiac event. I loved it –

"And then anger – that's so easy to create. It's the flip side of fear. If you can't flee, you have to fight. But if you can't fight, if you're tied down, if you're being tormented and abused, all you can do is burn with unrequited rage. Oh yes, I did that, too – I took you from resentment to rage and back again, over and over. I humiliated you and taunted you. I played you like a violin. Diapers and panties – those were just the warm-ups. What I did to your body, everything – it was a methodical campaign to strip you of your last pretense of masculinity. I stripped you as raw as a flayed corpse, just to feel the heat of your fury. And yes, you burned, you burned like the wrath of hell.

"Then – when you finally burned out, when there was absolutely nothing left to burn – I left you to grieve, to despair. I let you sink to the innermost depths of anguish and hysteria. You hung there, on the brink of insanity for the longest time. What bizarre hallucinations did you experience? Tiny spiders crawling inside your veins? Harpies shrieking into your ears as they ate your flesh? Eyeballs exploding out of your melting skull? Skin decomposing and falling away from your rotting corpse? What fun you must have had!

"And after that – when you finally resigned yourself to the contemplative hell of your captivity, that this was the shape of your death – that was when I began to tease and tickle you and take you on your journey of exquisite discovery, all designed to demonstrate the qualities of physical sensation available to a transformed body. I let you experience it as pleasure, as delight, as joyous rapture – and yes, I gave you access to an emotional repertoire that you had never known before. That should have sent you plunging even deeper into fear and anger and despair – the realization that you had wasted your life on brutality when this had always been available to you –

"But no, I wasn't going to send you there, that would have been cruel. And besides, it would have spoiled the flavor. No, I wanted you enthralled. I wanted you totally captivated by my power to control and manipulate you. I wanted that sweetness in your blood – and while it smacks of bragging, I think I accomplished it quite well. Despite my casual disparagement of your origins, you might very well become a worthwhile and respectable vintage. Time will tell. Please don't die on me now. Let your death take a long long time. Very long. I'm curious to see how well you'll age."

Jacob puts his hands behind his head and leans back against the headboard. "I kept him alive for three years, sipping a bit here, a bit there – until I realized that as good as he was, he wasn't going to get any better. So I ended him."

What my lover is talking about is so far beyond my experience, I don't know what to say. The best I can offer is a question. "Why? I mean, why didn't he get any better?"

"Depth."

"Depth?"

"He was incomplete. There was so much that he'd never experienced –"

"But you –"

Jacob faces me, his expression is intense. "It was my fault. I never let him out of the room. So he'd never had the opportunity to feed, never knew what it was like to capture and kill and celebrate the achievement of creating your own feast. You can't be a healthy predator without that skill. That's what was missing from his blood. He'd never had the chance to test the limits of his enhanced physical abilities. His body was vampire, but his blood wasn't. It had never been…finished."

I hadn't experienced that myself. Not yet. I wasn't sure what it would feel like. I could only imagine. I could only nod.

Jacob takes a deep breath and adds a final observation. "It was a useful experiment though."

"Useful?"

"Mm-hm. By learning what I was missing, I learned how to do it better the next time."

"Next time…?"

"Mm-hm…"

"But if you realized what was missing then, why didn't you let him out so he could be complete?"

"Because he was stupid." Jacob rolls to face me, pulls me into his arms, holds me close in a mutually cold embrace. "Being a successful vampire requires skill and training. It's not enough to be a sociopath, you also have to be intelligent and cunning and practical. Bud was none of these things. He was brutal and selfish and stupid. He would have become a monster. I don't want that kind of attention. None of us do."

I have nothing to say to that. His arms are cold, colder than mine. His heartbeat is slow and methodical – and eventually my heart synchronizes to his. I feel our blood, his and mine together, pulsing outward in mutually exciting waves. He smells delicious.

"Jacob?"

"Yes?"

"Can I ask you something?"

"You can ask me anything. I might answer…."

"Did you ever think of me that way?"

"What way?"

"You know what I mean."

He hesitates, then, "Yes, I considered it –"

"But…?"

"But nothing." He begins tracing his fingers along the curve of my chest, circling inward around my left nipple.

Author's Afterword

My first two years of college, I studied art and journalism. Both fields of study proved to be useful and important to me.

The journalism courses were practical experience in getting words onto paper. The goal was to write with precision, clarity, and accuracy. These are the most necessary skills for non-fiction, but they are also essential skills for storytelling.

We had to write — and we had to learn to write on demand. We had to learn how to write paragraphs that were informative and complete. The lesson to be learned — the paragraph is a skill. Every paragraph must function as a complete thought-cluster. Every sentence within the paragraph must move the thought forward to the next sentence.

The art courses took a different approach — they were experiential. What will you create? What can you learn by creating it?

One of the most powerful courses was an exploration of style.

On Monday of each week, we would study the style of a particular artist. Seurat looked at the world and saw it as multiple points of light. His canvases were not brush strokes, but pixels before the word was invented. Roualt painted strong colors with thick black lines outlining broad patches of color. Picasso (in his cubist period) broke the world into conflicting planes and flattened them onto the canvas. Henry Moore saw smooth bulbous shapes, many with holes in them. On Wednesday and Friday, we would draw or paint in that artist's specific style, looking at the world with that specific perception.

The lesson to be learned from that was profound. There was no right way to paint a picture. But neither was there any wrong way. The goal was to create a work that evoked a thought, a feeling, an emotion — a way of seeing the world.

At the time, I didn't see that as particularly useful to writing. I moved on. I studied film - at USC film school, the most important lessons were structure and editing. Actual hands-on experience with story or image is like finally getting a big glob of clay and molding it, discovering what can be done with it, what can't be done, and what can be alluded to because it can't be shown or told, only evoked.

At CSUN theater arts department, one of the most important lessons was the recognition of the audience. I picked up some acting experience. (I won't say I was great, maybe not even good, but I always knew my lines and I never bumped into the scenery.) But there was a lesson to be learned here as well — the actor has to get inside the character to create it.

And then — I sold that script to that TV series, and I was dropped head-first into the professional life.

Let me backtrack. In my first or second year in college, I took a creative writing course. About midway through the course, the instructor hauled me up in front of the class to berate me and tell me that I wasn't any good, that I was wasting my time and his, that I would never be a writer.

By the time I found out he was right, it was too late. I was making too much money, and I had a half-dozen award nominations. That was when I had to start learning how to be a writer.

There is this I have learned about myself. I do not like the word "can't." I hate the word "impossible." I see both those words as challenges. (Okay, striking a match on a bar of soap is impossible, that one I'll give you.)

At the beginning of my college career, I did not know how to write. That's why I took classes. The course that Irwin R. Blacker taught at USC taught me things about effective storytelling that transformed my experience at the keyboard. My experiences at CSUN taught me things about the nature of drama that transformed my relationships with my characters. Writing a character is analytical, but acting out a character's moments is experiential, and far more powerful for the creation of emotion.

That script to that TV series — that was analytical. It was a carefully contrived construction of plot and character and jokes. But it was also a learning experience.

Later, I began attending science fiction conventions and I had the opportunity to meet many of the authors who had informed my childhood and shaped my adolescence — men and women who had stretched the limits of possibility and expanded the event horizon of my imagination. I was privileged to meet and learn from Fred Pohl, Betty Ballantine, Harlan Ellison, Anne McCaffrey, James Blish, Hal Clement, Joanna Russ, Harry Harrison — and so many more.

But I still hadn't achieved mastery of the craft. Not in my mind. Despite some favorable reviews and a fair bit of positive acknowledgment, I still felt as if there was too much I did not yet know. (I was right about that.)

Mastery is a difficult concept to define. Even those who are recognized masters are often uneasy with the concept. (I know I am, and there are blurb writers who now describe me as "as master of the craft.") Even today, I am reluctant to discuss mastery for fear I will reveal that I still do not understand it. But I do recognize mastery when I see it created.

One of the questions I had been struggling with for the longest time was the concept of "style." Harlan Ellison had a style. Heinlein had a style. Both of those styles were immediately recognizable. But the idea of style was as slippery as that last sliver of soap in the bath tub ,and just as hard to catch when it escaped one's grasp.

During the seventies, I had several opportunities to hang out with Theodore Sturgeon. Sturgeon was widely considered to be one of the greatest authors and one of the finest stylists in the genre, and I was in awe of his insights and his skill. (Look up "A Saucer Of Loneliness," for example. It was his favorite of all his stories.)

One night, while a large group of us were gathered at a Westwood restaurant (following a Harlan Ellison sponsored lecture series), I asked Ted about style. He gave me the short course in metric-prose. (Write your sentences in a specific poetic meter to create a rhythm that evokes the emotion you want to create — staccato for action, lyrical and fluid for enchantment, intense for action, and so on.)

So, of course, I threw myself into metric prose as a way of mastering style. It was useful. It was important. It eventually morphed into a skill. The easier it is to speak a sentence aloud, the easier it is to read.

But I still hadn't mastered style — until one day, I realized that the word itself was a trap.

In its most common usage, style is fashion, something you put on one year and take off the next, replacing it with another style. This was especially true in the fifties and sixties, where clothing styles and automobile shapes were regularly redesigned in an obsessive-compulsive form of consumerism.

In literature, however, style is ... um, I dunno how to describe it, but I think I can point to it if somebody shows me what to point at.

Perhaps it was Sturgeon's Godbody that triggered the necessary insight. Each chapter in that book was voiced by a different character. And no matter which chapter you were reading, you always knew who was speaking, because that character's voice was so unique and so specific.

It wasn't style. It was voice.

To this day, I do not use the word style. (I still don't understand it.) But I am very clear about "voice."

Voice is the expression of the character. It's how the actor stands, gestures, speaks, and moves. It's the evocation of the soul. To write with a specific voice, the author must get inside the character, feel their physical being, feel their emotions, and see the world as they do. And then write from that experience.

Each of these three stories (I'll bet you were wondering if I'd ever get around to discussing them) required a serious investment of emotional energy. I had to dive deep into the characters before I could understand who they were, what they were feeling, how they were reacting to everything that was happening around them, and the choices they had to make. I had to become the people who were telling the story to find out where the story had to go.

If you've already read the stories, then you will have spent time with several unique individuals. Some were cruel. Some were humane. Some were no longer human. But each of them became very real to me in the writing -- and I hope they were equally real to you as you shared a few moments in their lives.

David Gerrold
July 2020

About The Author

David Gerrold

$\mathbf{D}$avid Gerrold's work is famous around the world. His novels and stories have been translated into more than a dozen languages. His TV scripts are estimated to have been seen by more than a billion viewers.

Gerrold's prolific output includes teleplays, film scripts, stage plays, comic books, more than 50 novels and anthologies, and hundreds of articles, columns, and short stories.

He has worked on a dozen different TV series, including *Star Trek*, *Land of the Lost*, *Twilight Zone*, *Star Trek: The Next Generation*, *Babylon 5*, and *Sliders*. He is the author of *Star Trek*'s most popular episode "The Trouble With Tribbles."

Many of his novels are classics of the science fiction genre, including *The Man Who Folded Himself*, the ultimate time travel story, and *When HARLIE Was One*, considered one of the most thoughtful tales of artificial intelligence ever written. His stunning novels on ecological invasion, *A Matter For Men*, *A Day For Damnation*, *A Rage For Revenge*, and *A Season For Slaughter*, have all been best sellers with a devoted fan following. His young adult series, The Dingilliad, traces the healing journey of a troubled family from Earth to a far-flung colony on another world. His Star Wolf series of novels about the psychological nature of interstellar war are in development as a television series.

A ten-time Hugo and Nebula award nominee, David Gerrold is also a recipient of the Skylark Award for Excellence in Imaginative Fiction, the Bram Stoker Award for Superior Achievement in Horror, and the Forrest J. Ackerman lifetime achievement award.

In 1994, Gerrold shared the adventure of how he adopted his son in *The Martian Child*, a semi-autobiographical tale of a science fiction writer who adopts a little boy, only to discover he might be a Martian. *The Martian Child* won the science fiction triple crown: the

Hugo, the Nebula, and the Locus Poll. It was the basis for the 2007 film *Martian Child* starring John Cusack and Amanda Peet.

Gerrold's greatest writing strengths are generally acknowledged to be his readable prose, his easy wit, his facility with action, the accuracy of his science, and the passions of his characters.   An accomplished lecturer and world-traveler, he has made appearances all over the United States, England, Europe, Canada, Australia, and New Zealand. His easy-going manner and disarming humor have made him a perennial favorite with audiences. David Gerrold was the Guest of Honor at the 2015 World Science Fiction Convention.

He is currently completing the fifth book in *The War Against The Chtorr* series.

About The Artist

M. D. Jackson

M.D. Jackson is a Canadian science fiction, fantasy and horror artist and illustrator. He has been drawing since he was old enough to hold a pencil.

His artwork has appeared on numerous book covers, and in the pages of various magazines including the current revival of *Amazing Stories*. His artwork has been used on the covers of books from Pulpwork Press, Rogue Blades Press and Rage Machine Books, among others, and recently from The Experimenter Publishing Company.

His work has been featured on various websites including Darkworlds Quarterly. He was the co-publisher of *Darkworlds Quarterly Magazine* which he maintains, a non-fiction online publication, providing illustrations as well as design and layout of each issue. He also wrote many of the articles about science fiction, fantasy and art. He wrote about similar subjects for the Amazing Stories Magazine Website, as well as at the now defunct Heroicology Website. Before that, he was the co-publisher and art director of *Dark Worlds m*agazine, a pulp inspired print-on-demand fiction magazine. His work garnered him a co-nomination for a Pulp Ark Award in 2012.

He works mainly in a digital medium. Happily, he is also handy with an ink pen and, of course, that old tested and true technology of the HB pencil and a scrap of paper.

M. D. Jackson lives among the tall Douglas Firs in a small town in the wild lands of the interior of British Columbia. He lives with his wife and two cats. When not working, he passes the time by drinking beer and reading old books.

M.D. Jackson
mdjackson.artstation.com

The World's First
Science Fiction Magazine

The latest iteration of Amazing Stories features fiction by some of the most renowned authors writing in the field of science fiction today, including Julie Czerneda, Paul Levinson, Alan Watt-Evans, Shirley Meier, Jack McDevitt, Paul Di Fillipo, David Gerrold and Allen Steele, as well as writers you may not know, but will want to read more of. The magazine also runs diverse columns on such subjects as current scientific knowledge and the writer's life. Fully illustrated, Amazing Stories is as enjoyable to look at as it is to read.

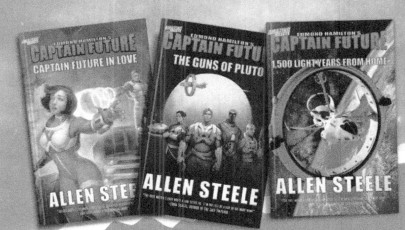

CAPTAIN FUTURE

The greatest space hero of science fiction's Golden Age, returns in this ALL NEW series of illustrated short novels written by multiple Hugo Award-winning author ALLEN STEELE, creator of the acclaimed Coyote series. Join Curt Newton and the Futuremen on an epic adventure that carries them from one side of the Solar System to the other... and beyond!

THE RETURN OF UL QUORN SERIES

BOOK 1 CAPTAIN FUTURE IN LOVE

BOOK 2 THE GUNS OF PLUTO

BOOK 3 1,500 LIGHT YEARS FROM HOME

COMING IN 2021 ... THE HORROR AT JUPITER

EPIC SPACE OPERA IN THE GRAND TRADITION!

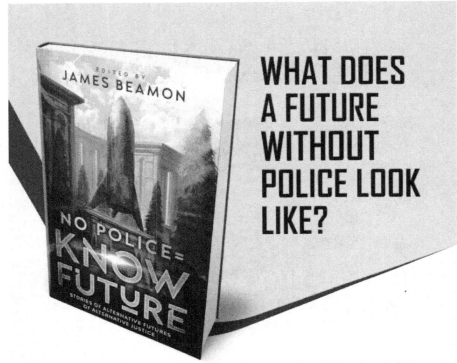

Made in the USA
Coppell, TX
12 May 2021

55574638R00105